THEY MOSTLY COME AT NIGHT

Collected Short Fiction

Wesley Southard

CEMETERY GATES
MEDIA

They Mostly Come at Night
Published by Cemetery Gates Media
Binghamton, New York

Copyright © 2022
by Wesley Southard

Introduction copyright © by Brian Keene

All rights reserved. Without limiting the rights under the copyright reserved above, no part of this publication may be reproduced, stored in, or introduced into a retrieval system, or transmitted in any form or by any means (electronic, mechanical, photocopying, recording, or otherwise) without prior written permission.

ISBN: 9798352144770

For more information about this book and other Cemetery Gates Media publications, visit us at:

cemeterygatesmedia.com
twitter.com/cemeterygatesm
instagram.com/cemeterygatesm

Cover Art: Trevor Henderson
Cover Design: www.CarrionHouse.com

*For Katie and Nolan
Mostly...*

"My Body" © 2020. First appeared in *Midnight in the Pentagram*, Silver Shamrock Publications.

"The Lengths I'll Go" © 2021. First appeared in *Sinister Magazine Issue 5*.

"Stuck" © 2022. Original to this collection.

"Separated Self" © 2022. Original to this collection.

"For You, Anything" © 2018. First appeared in *Clickers Forever: A Tribute to J. F. Gonzalez*, Thunderstorm Books and Deadite Press.

"Catalog" © 2019. First appeared in *Dig Two Graves Vol. 2*, Death's Head Press.

"Celebrity Mean Tweets" © 2022. Original to this collection.

"Echo" © 2021. First appeared in *Animali Fantastici e Come Salvarli*, Dunwich Edizioni. First published in the Italian language. This version is the first time it has been published in the English language.

"We Bare All" © 2020. First appeared in *One of Us: A Tribute to Frank Michaels Errington*, Bloodshot Books.

"Underneath" © 2022. Original to this collection.

"The Negative One" © 2021. First appeared in *Gorefest*, The Evil Cookie Publishing.

"Everyone is a moon, and has a dark side which he never shows to anybody."
— Mark Twain

"We're in some real pretty shit now, man!"
— Pvt. Hudson, *Aliens*

PRAISE FOR WESLEY SOUTHARD

"Southard's work bends the mind and punches the gut. His chilling tales offer all the carnage and chaos horror fanatics lick their chops for."

— Kristopher Triana, Splatterpunk Award-winning author of *Gone to See the River Man*

"Southard writes true blue-collar characters who are achingly real and endearing, and monsters that absolutely terrify. While one might note echoes of Richard Laymon, Southard's voice is all his own, and he uses it to deliver a compelling and powerfully enjoyable read."

— Mary SanGiovanni, author of *Beyond The Gate*

"Wesley Southard's writing thrums with uninhibited energy that's both infectious and entertaining. Discovering Wesley's work has been a joy, and you should seek out his books too. He's definitely a writer to watch."

— Jonathan Janz, author of *The Siren and the Spector* and *Exorcist Falls*

CONTENTS

Introduction by Brian Keene ... 9

My Body ... 13

The Lengths I'll Go ... 32

Stuck ... 47

Separated Self ... 49

For You, Anything ... 67

Catalog ... 77

Celebrity Mean Tweets ... 102

Echo ... 115

We Bare All ... 128

Underneath ... 149

The Negative One ... 151

Acknowledgements ... 161

THEY MOSTLY COME IN WAVES: AN INTRODUCTION BY BRIAN KEENE

If you asked me how many people I've signed books for over the years, I wouldn't be able to give you an exact number. It's certainly over 10,000 at this point, but after that, the math begins to hurt my head. It's impossible to remember all of those names, but I'm often surprised by how well I remember faces. When someone says, "Yeah, I met you at a signing in Ohio fifteen years ago and I reply with "I remember that" I'm not just being nice or bullshitting the person. I do, in fact, remember it. I remember every signing. The dates tend to jumble together into brain stew, but I remember the locations and the venues and the faces. Especially the faces.

Case in point—I remember the first time I signed books for Wesley Southard. I couldn't tell you what year it was, but he was young. In college I believe. Certainly barely out of high school. The signing took place in the basement of a church in Indiana—not the typical sort of place you'd expect to find myself, Wrath James White and Maurice Broaddus signing books, but there we were. I remember that Wes wore a black heavy metal t-shirt and asked good questions, and he had an expression of shell-shocked joy on his face as I signed his books and chatted with him. And then I sent him on his way.

Most of the time, that's the extent of these interactions. I write the books. People read the books. We meet in person at a signing and talk about the books. And then we go our separate ways. They're left feeling good that their favorite author wasn't an asshole and seemed genuinely pleased with their comments. And I'm left renewed, knowing that I'm not writing into the void, and that the things I write bring some joy to people's lives. That's a nice feeling. That's what it's all about. I try to remember that feeling when things get tough. And I remember the faces.

I didn't expect to see Wes's face again, so I was surprised and delighted when I did. I was even more surprised and delighted to learn that he was moving here, to my hometown, because he'd met and fallen in love with a Pennsylvania girl (his wife, Katie, who is wonderful and awesome and...yeah, he'd have been a fool not to move from Indiana to Pennsylvania for her). And I was surprised and delighted a third time when I found out that Wes wasn't just a reader. He wanted to become a writer.

And that was at least partially because of me, although Graham Masterton and J.F. Gonzalez also share some of the credit.

It has been my sincere pleasure to watch him develop as a writer over the last decade or so. I've mentored him when I could, advised him when he asked, and talked him off the ledge that all authors end up on throughout various times in their development and careers. I am proud of the formidable writer that Wes has become, as he now moves into position near the front of this new wave of horror.

At least once in every decade since the First World War, the public has had a renewed interest in horror fiction. In my book *Trigger Warnings*, I've broken this era of modern horror down into six waves.

That first wave, spanning from 1900 to the mid-1920s begins with the 1901 publication of M.P. Shiel's post-apocalyptic novel *The Purple Cloud*. That first wave of modern horror also gave us authors such as Lord Dunsany and William Hope Hodgson, and saw an increased public interest in ghost stories, particularly the work of M. R. James, Algernon Blackwood, and Edith Wharton (among others). 1923 brought us the birth of *Weird Tales*, a magazine whose long and varied history is so entwined with modern horror that it's as difficult to imagine the genre without it as it is to imagine the genre without Stephen King.

The second wave, spanning the mid-20s through the late-40s, was an important period that gave us H.P. Lovecraft, Frank Belknap Long, Robert E. Howard, Clark Ashton Smith, Shirley Jackson, and Seabury Quinn, among others, and the early works of Fritz Leiber.

The third wave, spanning the 1950s and 1960s gave us more mature works from Fritz Leiber, as well as the work of Anthony Boucher, Theodore Sturgeon, John Farris, Ira Levin, and five writers who are as important, if not more important, to the genre than even the works of the esteemed Mr. King—Robert Bloch, Richard Matheson, Ray Bradbury, Rod Serling, and the early works of Ramsey Campbell. These five writers were among the first to truly begin centering horror fiction in contemporary settings, rather than crumbling New England waterfront towns or sprawling Victorian mansions. Their impact and themes still inform much of today's horror fiction.

The beginning of the fourth wave—the 1970s and 1980s, brought us Stephen King, Dean Koontz, F. Paul Wilson, Thomas

Monteleone, Karl Edward Wagner, Peter Straub, and others. When King became a bestseller in paperback, the marketing category of HORROR was invented. The genre waned briefly around 1979-1980 but then came back with a vengeance. The 4th wave also gave us Clive Barker, Charles L. Grant, James Herbert, TED Klein, Robert R. McCammon, Joe R. Lansdale, Jack Ketchum, Richard Laymon, Rick Hautala, Ronald Kelly, the Splatterpunks, Brian Hodge, and Poppy Z. Brite. This era also saw the early works of such current luminaries as Edward Lee and Tom Piccirilli.

My generation—typified by writers such as Mary SanGiovanni, Joe Hill, Christopher Golden, Tim Lebbon, Jonathan Maberry, Paul Tremblay, Stephen Graham Jones, Carlton Mellick, Jeff Vandermeer, Bryan Smith, Sarah Pinborough, Maurice Broaddus, Weston Ochse, JF Gonzalez, Wrath James White, Tom Piccirilli, Sarah Langan, Nick Mamatas, and many more—make up the fifth wave. We rose to prominence in the first decade of this new century. We were the first generation to have the Internet. We bridged the gap between the fourth wave—authors who had to adapt to new technology—and the sixth wave, the post-internet generation.

The sixth wave are now cresting in prominence, inspiring the forthcoming seventh wave who will begin to emerge a few years from now, and that is a wonderful thing to see. And it does my heart good to see Wesley Southard riding at the top of that swell and helping to lead that charge. Those kids in the forthcoming seventh wave don't know how lucky they are to have him.

But this collection is a good indicator. These are stories by an author who has found his voice and grown confident (but not cocky) with his craft. Stories by an author who loves this genre, who knows its rich history, and who has something important to say. He's not just paying homage to Graham Masterton or J.F. Gonzalez or myself anymore. He's at the top of his game, and soon, he will sign a book for some youngster, and he will remember their face, if not their name, and they will go home and be inspired and write a Wesley Southard homage. Trust me when I tell you, there's no better feeling as a writer than to know you've helped make that happen.

An addendum before I finish up here. As I write this, I've just come from yet another convention where books got signed all weekend long. At one point, Wrath James White and I were staring out across the room, and ruminating on all of the physical maladies that come with getting past the age of fifty. At one point, we glanced over at Wes's table, and he was signing a book for somebody, and I asked Wrath if he remembered the first time we'd met Wes, in the basement of that church. Wrath did a double take, and then turned to me and whispered, "Brian, we're the old guys now."

And I smiled and nodded at Wes and said, "Yeah, we are. but the genre is in good hands."

Now, let's surf that wave with Wes, and see where he takes us.

I hope you wore a bathing suit because there's wet work ahead...

— Brian Keene
Somewhere along the Susquehanna River
April 2022

MY BODY

Meat cleaver in hand and her belly full of blood, Cynthia hid beneath the carving table, trembling in fear. Not only was the ice-cold blood drying on her blouse and face, it rippled uncomfortably inside her. The red across her palms refused to dry, her skin slick with sweat, and the heavy, rectangular blade repeatedly slipped from her grip. Eyes blurred with tears, she curled into herself, terrified this day would never come to an end.

Outside, insistent fists continued to beat on the front door.

**

"You know, Mrs. Owen, I've been at this a long time—a *very* long time—and in all my years of being a restaurant proprietor, I've never been sent such a *beautiful* reporter to cover any of my establishments."

There it is, Cynthia thought, miserably. *Only three minutes in and I'm already being hit on.* At this point in her career, she felt like she should have been used to it, but every time a tasteless compliment or slick one-liner barged in and sat right dead on her lap, it still pissed her off. She was a professional and expected to be treated as such.

Par for the course, she supposed.

The man in the slick Brioni pinstripe suit, Jermane Welkner, shot her a toothy grin full of affluential confidence. There was no chance he had purchased that seven thousand dollar bragging right here in *this* town. He may have been loaded, but she doubted he came to work on a normal day dressed to the nines. Today, he came to impress. From behind his polished oak desk, the man oozed confidence.

Cynthia shot him a tight-lipped smile. "Let's focus, shall we, Mr. Welkner?"

He presented his hands in surrender. "My apologies, Mrs. Owen. Sometimes I just can't help myself."

"It's *Ms.* Owen."

"*Oh?*"

"So, it says here in my research you own...twenty-one restaurants, with *Mon Corps* being number twenty-two. Your eateries are spread across fifteen states, many of varying fare, though most are in the upper tier of price point. Suit and tie affairs."

"Sounds about right."

Cynthia scanned her notes. "According to Forbes, you're said to have a net worth of nearly six million, and you have a house in nearly every state you have an establishment."

Welkner nodded, adjusting his tie. "Impressive research, *Ms.* Owen."

"What's really impressive, Mr. Welkner, is what you've managed to do with this building. I'm sure you already know, but this particular site has housed nearly ten other restaurants over the last thirty years since the original building was constructed. No matter what the place served—Mexican, Italian, Japanese, Indian—it failed to draw interest and ceased operations. Nothing has ever stayed here for more than six months tops. And somehow you come strolling in with, of all things, a high-end French bistro, and you take the town by storm."

The older man glowed with pride. "Indeed."

"So why here? Why Evansville, Indiana, a city of barely one hundred and twenty thousand people, and not in Indianapolis or Fort Wayne, places where the population is dramatically higher and diversity is better celebrated. This city has always had a deep German heritage, but at the end of the day, it barely holds onto its single German restaurant. I'm sure you're aware you're in the middle of chain restaurant heaven, where it's far easier to feed a family on a middle-class budget. So why French cuisine? Why here?"

"These questions seem awfully peculiar, Ms. Owen. Am I under oath here?"

She waved him off. "Not at all. I'm only here to write a short piece about the abrupt success of *Mon Corps* and to have a taste of your fine food as part of my article."

"A food blogger?"

"Not quite. I'm employed by the Courier Press, not as an independent."

"And how does one become the local paper's food tester?"

Cynthia bit the inside of her cheek to keep herself from throwing her notebook at Welkner's waxy, product-heavy face. "Well, long story short, I failed out of culinary school and moved back home from New York and needed a job. Not having the heart to rejoin a kitchen staff, I saw the paper was willing to pay someone to test and grade new restaurants and do write ups on whether or not I would recommend the new kids in town."

Welkner cocked a teasing eyebrow. "And do we pass, Ms. Owen? Are we *cool* enough for this school?"

"That remains to be seen. How's the food?"

Laughing, Welkner smiled and pointed at her. "I like you, Cynthia—may I call you Cynthia? You can call me Jermane. In fact, I prefer it."

"Ms. Owen is fine. And you still haven't answered my question."

"Which was?"

Cynthia inwardly rolled her eyes. "Why are you the only one that stuck?"

Welkner leaned back in his chair, hands linked behind his head. "It's quite simple, actually: I have an eye for what works and what doesn't. Much like all of my other establishments, I saw an opportunity, so I pounced on it. It's like this... McDonald's doesn't just sell two billion burgers a year by accident. They're not so much of a burger joint as they are a brilliant real estate company. They always know the *exact* right place in every single town they lay brick down on to open up their grease traps. Turn that way, a McDonald's—turn back behind you, another damn McDonald's. I noticed that early on in my career, and I took that strategy to heart. Each one of my twenty-two restaurants, including this fine building we are sitting in, are located in the very best area of that chosen city, and if they aren't already standing, like this one, I buy the land and build it. Not only do I serve the finest food at my restaurants, I have the eyes of everyone in town, whether they can afford it or not. Middle class or lower, they'll find the means to dine with me."

Cynthia hated to admit it, but this was going to make for an interesting article.

"As far as it being French," he continued, "this is a new venture for me. I blame that on Alex."

"That's Alexandre Boucher, correct?"

"Correct. He searched me out, and we found this town and this building. His food is quite delectable, and it's caught the appetite of all the local...what are Indiana residents called again?"

"Hoosiers."

"That's it. It's just that straightforward. This town was dying for a taste of Europe they've never experienced, and we're giving them what they want."

"You certainly are, Mr. Welkner. From what I gather, your sales have doubled, sometimes tripled, nearly every week since you opened two months ago."

He grinned smugly. "If you try the *Bouillabaisse*, you'll understand why."

"I plan on it." Cynthia closed her notebook and stood. "In fact, I plan on sampling most of the dishes here tonight. Can't give a proper evaluation if I don't."

Welkner rose with a grunt. "And I will make sure you receive the best service possible. You'll be sitting at my personal dining room table."

As they exited the office, the heat of the kitchen hit her like two hands to the chest. Kitchen staff hustled and bustled in their crisp white uniforms and hats, cutting, slicing, mixing, and mashing. The inviting aroma of frying duck and spiced sausages permeated the air, mingling with the rich scents of sage and tarragon, instantly making her mouth water. The feeling didn't come often, but when it did, she missed the rush of a bustling kitchen on a hectic Friday night.

She turned back to Welkner. "Would you mind if I spoke to Mr. Boucher for a moment? I'd like to get a few quotes for the article."

Welkner shrugged. "That's not up to me. I'll take you to him, but he's not much of a talker, especially when he's in the zone. Let's go see if he's up to it."

A quick walk up the far side of the kitchen, and they faced the frenzy of the front line. A half a dozen men and women worked the grills and ovens, each one sweating in silence. A young woman, who Cynthia assumed was the sous-chef, worked shoulder to shoulder with a much older man in an almost comically tall chef's hat. His thick black mustache and eyebrows gleamed with perspiration as he intently worked on plating an order of *Salmon en papillote*.

Dodging the busy waiters, she stepped around to the other side of the heated pass window. "Mr. Boucher? Mr. Boucher, my name is Cynthia Owen. I'm a reporter and food critic for the Courier Press. I'm doing an article about your restaurant and would like to speak to you for a moment, if I could."

Without moving his head, Boucher lifted his eyes slightly and glanced at her, then returned to his work just as quickly.

"You've got quite the setup here, Mr. Boucher. I'm rather impressed."

"*Merci.*"

"Is it always this busy on Fridays?"

He remained focused on his work, handing the plate to his sous-chef before grabbing another from the grill chef behind him. "*Oui.*"

She could already tell this was going nowhere. "I, um, I learned a bit about the start of the restaurant from Mr. Welkner, but I still have a few more questions. The name of the place, *Mon Corps*. Why exactly did you choose to name it 'My Body'? Seems like an odd name, wouldn't you say?"

He remained silent, carefully placing diced tomatoes onto a plate of chicken confit. Then he muttered, "French food is good for body. For soul. Hearty. Delicious. Makes people happy."

Cynthia nodded. "Okay, that makes sense. And I have to agree. I'm a big fan of French cuisine. I just have one more question. I did a bit of research before I came here tonight, and I cannot seem to find any information about you out there at all. I asked around and made some phone calls, but no one has ever heard of you, Mr. Boucher. Where exactly did you come from before partnering with Mr. Welkner?"

The kitchen line stopped moving. The grill cooks all turned to look at her with blank expressions. The young sous-chef side-eyed her boss. With a frown, Alexandre Boucher lifted his head and glared at her. The sudden silence made her shiver.

Without a word, Boucher grabbed two empty meat containers from the chiller in front of him and a large carving blade and exited the line. With several long strides, he skulked to the back of the kitchen. He then unlocked a thick metal door with a key attached to his belt and stepped inside a dark room, slamming the door shut behind him.

Welkner placed a hand on her shoulder. "See? Not much of a talker, but a whiz of a cook."

Cynthia swallowed as she stared at the back door. "That's okay." She turned to face him. "Might I ask, where does that door lead to?"

"To a sub-basement. It wasn't here before we moved in. Boucher insisted we have it built. It's where he stores a lot of the food, mostly the meats. Something about the natural coolness of the earth or whatnot. All I know is it cost me a damn fortune, and he won't even let me down there to see what I paid for. Anyway, enough chatting. Let's get you seated."

"That sounds good, but I'll find it on my own. My boyfriend is probably already at the table waiting for me."

Welkner seemed to shrivel. "A boyfriend? You're breaking my heart, Ms. Owen."

"If the food isn't good, I'll really break your heart on page five tomorrow."

***

The front doors to the restaurant crashed open. From underneath the carving table, Cynthia stifled a scream and gripped the meat cleaver tighter. Footsteps scattered throughout the dining room. A moment later, the kitchen doors swung inward.

***

Grunting, Cynthia fell back onto her pillow. Above her, Greg followed suit, collapsing onto his side of the bed with an exhausted sigh. Both were drenched in sweat, both waiting for their breaths to find them again.

"Holy shit," her boyfriend stuttered.

"Yeah."

"Like, *holy shit!*"

"I know."

Greg wiped his face. "What the hell got into us?" He began to laugh. "I'm so damn full I could burst, and all I could think of on the way back was how bad I wanted to get home and jump into bed with you. Is that crazy?"

Cynthia grinned and laughed, as well. "Hand me that towel." After tossing her the washcloth, she began to wipe off her bare stomach—a stomach full of quite possibly the best food she had ever eaten. Dozens of delectable samples of *Coq au Vin*, *Cassoulet*, and *potatoes Dauphinoise*. A steaming bowl of *Boeuf Bourguignon*. A hearty slice of *Quiche Lorraine*. The lamb chops—*my God*, *those lamb chops!* They ended the meal with chocolate drizzled *Profiteroles* and a *mousse* so rich it hurt her teeth. For all the doubt she had going in, Welkner definitely put his money where his mouth was. Part of her wanted to shred the arrogant prick in her review, but with the immense satisfaction buzzing through her body—not to mention the great, spontaneous sex she and Greg had the moment they came back home—the place would receive probably the best score she'd given out in her eight years on the job.

Never in all that time had she continued to think about the food long after she ate it. Hours after Greg finally fell asleep, Cynthia sat awake, staring at the ceiling…wishing she could get another taste. It was absolutely incredible. Every dish, every single bite was like a little slice of perfectly-cooked heaven. She could only dream of being able to prepare food like that, which was the exact reason she couldn't cut it in Hyde Park and had to move back to the Midwest with her tail between her legs. No matter how well she was doing now, it was always her biggest regret, and seeing firsthand what she could have been brought back the same feeling of shame she felt all those years ago. If she wasn't worth a damn in the kitchen, she could damn well help others be.

In the dark, she pulled out her laptop and did a little more digging on Alexandre Boucher. Once again, she came up empty. Not a single article, not a solitary shred of back story. She knew most chefs to be eccentric and outgoing, always searching for the limelight, but to have one as talented as Boucher presumably appear from thin air was disorienting. This was a first for her, and for some reason she couldn't let it go.

She closed the laptop, then her eyes, and dreamt of warm meat.

***

They scrambled into the kitchen by the dozens, their footsteps erratic and purposeful. All around her various metal instruments hit the concrete floor as the crazies tore the room apart, tossing aside anything not already anchored down. Underneath the carving table, she curled in tighter, carefully shifting two large plastic mixing tubs so they would better hide her.

***

Sitting at her desk, Cynthia couldn't concentrate. Her head throbbed, and her stomach ached deeply. It was only 10:00 a.m., and everyone around her was grating on her nerves. Questions and answers, sign this, approve that, look at these—*shut the fuck up!* She liked to think of herself as a fairly easy-going, happy person, but she couldn't shake this enduring annoyance of everyone around her. People she'd known for years, who she considered her closest friends, were now like flies constantly landing on her face.

What the hell is wrong with me?

She knew what was wrong, and she didn't care to admit it. It was embarrassing that she couldn't stop thinking about *Mon Corps*. She was a professional, and the fact she continued to obsess about food she had eaten over a week ago made Cynthia want to bang her head against a wall. She should have been preparing for tonight's assignment, a new Mexican restaurant opening over in Newburgh. Instead, she found herself daydreaming about *cordon bleu* and *Magret de canard*. She typically didn't double dip into past eateries, specifically those she reviewed for work, but the thought of not tasting Boucher's *Tête de veau* again drove her absolutely crazy. She had to know more about the man and his food. Perhaps...she would go again.

Cynthia's cell rang. "Greg? Everything okay?"

"It most certainly *isn't* fucking okay. I just got fired!"

"What do you mean *fired*?"

Greg laughed sarcastically. "Fired, Goddamn it! I finally had enough of Morrison's shit, so I punched him right in the nose! You should have seen it. Blood went everywhere!"

Cynthia sat up straight. "Wait—you *hit* your boss?"

"I don't know what came over me, Cyn. He started mouthing off again this morning, and I just...*snapped*. I hit him in front of everyone at the plant."

"Christ Almighty, Greg!"

"And that's not even the best part."

She pulled a face. "*The best part?*"

"The moment he hit the ground, I straddled him and just started *whaling* on him. It took, like, three co-workers to pull me off of him. Well, I guess they're not co-workers anymore. I assume I'm shitcanned."

"Greg, that's terrible!"

"Screw it. I'm heading home. I don't feel like meeting you in Newburgh for dinner. Just go on your own, okay?"

Before she could answer, he hung up. She sat there for a little while longer, staring at her computer and the lack of answers Google provided about Boucher.

Yes…perhaps she *would* go again.

Hours later, while she gorged herself in a corner booth at *Mon Corps*, in a dining room packed to the gills with enthusiastic, hungry patrons, Cynthia saw Greg sneak in and pick up a take-out order at the front desk.

***

A woman screamed and darted across the kitchen. Cynthia assumed she was part of the janitorial staff, hiding just like her, and had stayed there while Cynthia raided the kitchen. The terrified woman ran for the back door in a panic.

In a flash, the crazies tackled the woman to the ground. While she kicked and screamed, they grasped her by the quarters and lifted. The woman screamed and cried in horror. The crazies laughed and laughed. Once they had a solid grip, they walked her across the room toward Cynthia's table and slammed her down on the polished steel surface. Hiding beneath, Cynthia gripped the cleaver tight.

Dozens of legs surrounded her. The woman's feet stomped on the tabletop above Cynthia. Butcher's knives in hand, the crazies continued their hysterical laughter as they rained their sharpened blows down on the woman. Like her screams, her struggles eventually diminished. Bright red blood spilled over the sides of the surface and raced down the table legs, splashing the floor.

Heart pounding, Cynthia carefully reached out amidst the chaos and smeared some on her hand. She popped a wet finger into her mouth.

The thing growing inside of her thanked her.

***

It had been three days since she'd heard from Greg and nearly a week since she'd even seen him…and for some reason, it was the last thing she cared about. She had confronted him that night after seeing him at *Mon Corps*. He denied it to her face. They shouted back and forth, calling each other liars. When the subject of being out of work came up, he snapped and hit her. She hadn't expected it, his strike swift as a snake bite. And he laughed.

He fucking laughed.

While he was cackling like a maniac, Cynthia snatched the letter opener from her home office desk and shoved the dull blade into his thigh.

Then she, too, started laughing.

Shocked, Greg screamed and hobbled out of the house, and she hadn't heard a peep from him since. The pain she caused him, the sudden act of violence toward her partner, made her feel sick...but something deep down in her guts told her it was the right thing to do. It spoke to her in whispered words. It *thanked* her.

Pushing the voice away, she sat behind her desk at work and continued her online search for information on Boucher. Every corner she could scour, every site dedicated to international chefs, continued to come up empty. Frustration was beginning to build, and everyone around her purposely stayed clear. A small part of her wanted them to get close, to annoy the shit out of her so she would have an excuse to strike. She was beginning to think Greg had the right idea. Instead, she listened to their background chatter as they gabbed about their weekends and family gatherings. More than a few times, she heard mention of *Mon Corps*.

Instead of searching for Boucher's background, she did some digging on the actual building the restaurant occupied. Built in 1991, it was originally designed for a national Tex-Mex chain, but after several dozen people got sick from undercooked food, the restaurant shamefully closed its doors. Not even six months later, a local couple bought it and opened their dream pizza joint, only to see it fail due to lack of interest. The building remained closed for nearly a year after that before being sold to another company, an upscale East Coast seafood micro chain, wanting to test the waters in the Midwest. When the waters proved too cold, they packed up and left, allowing for six more eateries to give it the old college try. All failures.

So damn strange. How is it possible nothing caught on?

Her research only got weirder. When she went to find any info on the previous owners, what she discovered was shocking. Despite their age and health, every single one of them was now dead, having passed away not long after their restaurants closed. Cynthia sat back and stared at her computer screen in bewilderment. That couldn't be right. And yet, every obituary she dug up only added to her confusion.

Like it was destined to be Mon Corps...

A hand on her shoulder startled her back to reality. Her line-editor, Mary Sestero, was glaring over her with a sneer. "Cynthia, what the hell is wrong with you? You were supposed to go to Newburgh last week, and instead you hand me another fluff article about that damn French place? Care to explain yourself?"

Bleed. Make her bleed.

Cynthia had no idea where the voice came from, but she obliged it. She quickly stood and backhanded the woman across the face. Mary stumbled back, holding her wide-eyed, shocked face. Blood trickled out of her nose. Cynthia, just as shocked as Mary, stared her down.

Something thick and heavy coiled around in her stomach. This time it said, *Again. More blood.*

Mary staggered away. The rest of her co-workers were frozen in stunned surprise.

Now. More blood. Now.

"No…"

Feed me.

"*No!*" she screamed.

The large plate glass window overlooking the upstairs lobby exploded. A man Cynthia didn't recognize leapt through the opening. Pistol in hand, he howled with laughter as he opened fire on the office. Blood bloomed across the white walls as her co-workers screamed and collapsed, each of them now full of dime-sized holes. Since her desk was so close to the back stairwell, Cynthia quickly ducked out of the room and down the steps. Heart racing, she ran through the car park, hopping over several other dead bodies on the way, and found her car. She winced as dozens of random gunshots popped outside of the building. Some were far away. Others were much closer. Screams and maniacal laughter filled the air.

Hoping to find Greg, Cynthia raced home, all while the lump in her stomach begged for more blood.

***

The poor woman above her had completely stopped moving, and it was easy to see why. The crazies surrounding the table danced joyously in the pool of fluid they had created on the kitchen floor. Cynthia knew she should be revolted, but the copper taste on her tongue reminded her she was no saint.

Then the crazies stopped. In unison, they turned. The back storage door slowly creaked open, revealing an empty black maw beyond. As if by instinct, they shuffled through the open door, disappearing beyond.

As they exited the room, one of the crazies slipped in the blood in front of her table and collapsed to the floor. The man sat up on his elbows and turned toward Cynthia.

Greg grinned at her with blood-stained teeth.

***

Traffic was a literal nightmare. Cynthia weaved between dozens of stalled cars, manned and unmanned. Pileup after pileup. Smoke and gunshots. People being pulled out of their houses and stabbed repeatedly in the streets. Faces shredded by fingers. Men, women, and children—no one was spared. It seemed as though the whole town had gone crazy, and if the voice coming from her gut held any sort of sway, she'd be right there with them.

Hands shaking with adrenaline, she pulled to a screeching stop in front of her house.

Cynthia stared in horror.

Greg, the man she once considered the love of her life, was repeatedly beating their neighbor and his twelve-year-old daughter on their lawn with an aluminum bat. The girl's head was almost gone, bones and brains mashed into a sloppy pink soup. Sweat dripping down his blood-speckled face, Greg looked up at Cynthia and laughed.

"What do you think, baby? French sound good tonight?"

Greg hobbled toward the car.

Cynthia hit the gas.

***

"How about it, Cyn?" Greg rasped, sitting up on his knees. "Have we done enough sinning yet?"

"Stay away!" Cynthia kicked the mixing bucket at Greg, who quickly batted it away. She swung the cleaver at him, warding him off. "Don't you fucking touch me!"

"Don't be like that, baby... It's all over now. We did exactly what it asked."

"W-what are you talking about?" she asked, still swinging the blade.

Greg smiled wide, unbuttoning the polo collar around his throat. "Let it take you over, Cyn. Feed it and add to its body." He winked. "Help him live again."

His body spasmed into an uncontrollable shake. Greg pitched forward on his hands, groaning in pain. Blood spurted from his lips. Eyes wide, he threw his head back and, giving one last hoarse scream, his throat bulged and exploded. Cynthia cried out as something long and dark red hit the floor with a wet, mushy slap. Greg's lifeless body collapsed on its side.

Cynthia gazed in horror as the long piece of meat reared up like a snake and slithered off toward the back storage door.

***

With nowhere to go, Cynthia drove to the only place that made any sense to her. The answers she sought were at *Mon Corps*, and at this point, she would kill to get those answers.

Kill. Kill. Kill.

"Shut up!"

Though it was closed on Mondays, she wouldn't let that stop her from getting inside. Adding to the chaos around her, she used the lug wrench she kept in her trunk to pop open the front door. She stepped inside, then relocked and barricaded the door behind her with the couch from the front lobby. No alarm sounded at her intrusion.

"Alexandre Boucher!" she yelled to the empty black dining room. "Where are you, you son of a bitch?" When no one answered, she sprinted into the kitchen. "What the hell have you done to us? What's in your food?" She flicked on the lights and found the kitchen similarly deserted.

Then the smell hit her. All the food. All the scents. All the spices. All the *meat*.

Feed me.

Cynthia's eyes blurred, head cocked.

Feed. Me.

Her senses overpowered her. Before she knew what she was doing, she dashed for the freezer locker near the salad station and threw open the door. She inhaled deeply, letting her nose drive her legs.

In the back corner of the freezer, a few buckets of chilled meat sat on a metal rack. Without thinking, she dove for the nearest bucket and dug her fists into the raw meat, smashing as much of it as she could into her mouth. The voice inside her stomach moaned with excitement as Cynthia lifted the bucket and drank the icy blood within. Being a longtime cook, she was confident in her ability to identify just about any type of protein offered to her—not to mention the fact it was part of her culinary school curriculum—but she had never tasted anything like this. And now that she had it dripping in her mouth, she could tell this was the very meat used in nearly every dish at the restaurant. Maybe it was prepared in different ways, mixed with different spices and ingredients, but the tang—the *potency*—was utterly indistinguishable.

What are you, you delectable monster?

The bucket now empty, the lump inside her guts sang with glee. Cynthia dropped the bucket and stumbled backwards toward the door, now feeling the weight of what she'd just done. Disgusted, she re-entered the warmth of the kitchen and ran for the sink, jabbing two fingers down her throat.

More blood. More.

Before she could expel the contents of her stomach, countless angry fists erupted against the front door of the restaurant.

***

After the raw, red thing had burst from Greg's body and slithered out of the room, Cynthia slowly crawled out from under the carving table. Keeping the blade tight in her grip, she carefully stepped over Greg's nearly-decapitated head and followed the trail of slimy blood toward the open back door. She turned back, quickly checking the rest of the kitchen for crazies, and then stepped through the doorway.

The door slammed shut behind her.

Smothered in black, Cynthia quickly remembered her cell phone. She pulled it out and shook it, activating the flashlight. She expected some sort of walk-in freezer, one big enough for hundreds of pounds of Boucher's meat, but the sudden brightness simply revealed a long, dark hallway that didn't appear to end. Beneath her feet, bloody footprints and a wide, slimy trail led down the path.

Carefully, she tottered down the narrow walkway. The further she traversed, the more the floor sloped downward. Soon, the warm summer air disappeared, replaced by the crisp, natural bite of deep earth. She imagined she was now somewhere underneath the expressway, across the restaurant's parking lot. Welkner really had no idea what he paid for.

Eventually, the hallway came to an end. A carved dirt doorway opened up before her. Cold, inky black rested beyond.

Trembling, Cynthia stepped through.

The room was cavernous and hollow like a carved-out gourd. Lifting her arm, she swept her flashlight back and forth. Beneath her feet, hundreds upon hundreds of fresh dead bodies lay face-down on the dirt-packed floor. Similar to Greg, their throats had been the means of escape for the sludgy red creature gestating in their stomachs—presumably the same thing egging her on. Just looking at them made the thing inside her wriggle with excitement.

The hushed sound of their slithering filled the room.

Gingerly, she stepped around the bodies and continued to arch her light. Her beam caught something in the far corner.

Cynthia gasped.

In the wide circle of light, a massive body sat slumped against the wall. At least fifteen feet high, there wasn't much left to the being—*whatever* it was. Its bones were yellowed with age and mildew. Its skull was the size of a buffalo's, with a wide-set, razor-toothed mouth that reached well to the back of its neck. Two sizable horns curled up from its temples. Cynthia knew she should be terrified, knew damn well what she was looking at, but she felt…fascination. Wonder. Sadness.

A large hand fell onto her wrist. Cynthia shrieked, nearly dropping her phone. Boucher stood next to her in the dark, watching her with a curious eyebrow. He was still dressed in his white chef's smock, complete with his oversized hat. With his other hand, he snatched the blade from her hand and tossed it into the darkness.

"Pitiful, isn't it?"

Cynthia stared at him, wondering where his French accent had gone.

"He was such a beautiful boy." Boucher frowned sadly at the massive corpse.

She whispered, "What is it?"

"My heir."

"I...I don't understand."

"Where we stand, my dear, is old, hallowed ground. You wouldn't fathom the atrocities which occurred in this very place, long before man stepped foot in this world. To do so would drive you mad. I owned this land, every nook and cranny. Then your beloved God created you wriggling fissures, and you set your hooks in and destroyed everything I created. You people slayed my baby boy and buried his corpse as if he were nothing more than a mutt's fecal matter."

Boucher's grip tightened on her wrist. What little light from her phone that reached his hand showed his fingers had lengthened by several inches and flushed to a deep ruby red. Cynthia sensed him growing taller beside her. She kept her eyes locked onto the rotted skeleton ahead. They lingered on the small strips of petrified meat still clinging to the bones. Her mouth began to water.

The thing beside her leaned into her ear. "Tasty, wasn't he?"

Feed me. Feed me.

Cynthia wretched.

Boucher cackled. "No part of him went to waste, and no one could deny his power. You're all so predictable. Like little piggies, you'll fill your greedy mouths with anything, not even thinking twice about it. And for that, I am eternally grateful."

Boucher continued to grow taller, wider. The slithering grew louder.

"A millennia of searching led me here, back to my missing child. But no tears. This is not a sad occasion—quite the opposite. You see, like all other creations, everything's perennial. A prince can never really die. He sleeps..." Still gripping her hand, he gradually moved the flashlight's beam until it faced the opposite wall. "...waiting to be remade."

Cynthia screamed.

A massive red figure filled the dull light of her phone. It sat with its legs straight out, filling up the entire corner of the room. Sucking in deep, hissing breaths through its nose, the prince's eyes glared down at them. It held its large, paw-like hands out in beckon. Among the corpses, the long, mushy pieces of meat slithered across the floor, then up his arms, legs, and across his trunk. The demon's fresh parts absorbed into his new, hulking body. Each one he soaked in sent pleasurable shivers rippling through his bright red hide.

"What a handsome boy!" Boucher declared.

When the last of the demon's parts climbed him and became his new flesh, his black snake-slit eyes turned downward. Numb and shaking, Cynthia gawked up at him, noticing the absence of a mouth on his face.

The voice inside her stomach raged: *Kill! Kill! Blood! Blood!*

"It's all down to you, dear Cynthia." The thing that was once Alexandre Boucher released her wrist and stepped out from behind her.

Much like his son, the demon towered over her with daunting intimidation. Horns raging high over his head, his wide, razor-toothed mouth grinned at her. Much like his human form, he appeared far older than she could have ever guessed, but that didn't mean he was any less threatening.

"You know what you must do," Boucher said.

The demon snapped his fingers, and Jermane Welkner came flying out of the darkness. He screamed as he tumbled over the dead bodies near her feet. Before he could jump to his own and run, the elder demon grabbed him by the back of his head and lifted him into the air.

"Let me go! Let me go, Goddamn you!"

The demon scowled. "God damned me eons ago, worm! Defiance and will to conquer Heaven will do that, even to his most loved creation." He turned to Cynthia. "It's all up to you, my dear. Give my son his voice back. Complete him. Let him be whole again and fulfill his birthright. My time is done. It's his turn to rise up and rule. I ask you, let an old, dispossessed seraph finally die."

Shaking uncontrollably, Cynthia's eyes darted back and forth between the two, unsure what to do. Her brain and heart told her to run, to get as far away from all this death and madness as she could. But her stomach raged like a hurricane over choppy waters.

KILL! KILL! BLOOD! BLOOD!

Cynthia flexed her hands.

She glanced up at the giant, mouthless prince awaiting her answer. His glassy eyes pleaded.

"No!" Welkner cried. "Please, Mrs. Owen! Please don't hurt me!"

Cynthia gritted her teeth, feeling the rage wash over her. "It's…*Ms*…Owen!"

In a flash, she dropped her phone and leapt forward, driving her thumbs directly into Welkner's eyes. The older man screamed. He kicked and lashed out with frantic fists, but Cynthia leaned into him and continued to push as hard as she could. Blood ruptured from his eye sockets and sprayed across her face. Cynthia laughed, relishing the glee that now coursed through her body. The voice inside her stomach squealed with pleasure. When it seemed her thumbs could go no further, she gave them another thrust, and they dug even deeper into the man's head. Welkner wailed the entire time, and Cynthia continued to cackle.

A few minutes later, she released her hands. The elder demon dropped Welkner's corpse, adding it to the countless others.

"How did that feel, Cynthia?"

She wiped the joyful tears from her eyes. "Delightful."

Grinning, he stepped back into the darkness, disappearing from the light. "It's now your time, my son."

With a grunt, the massive prince stood. Cynthia dropped to her knees before him. Hands holding her cheeks, manic laugher erupted from her throat, and a few moments later so did the rest of the new king.

Story Notes:

Much like the story suggests, there is indeed a real restaurant in Evansville, Indiana that, when I was growing up, rotated tenants fairly often. Pretty strange for a primo spot right off the expressway, sandwiched between two other chain restaurants that have never left their spots. The writer in me had always wondered why that was. So when the opportunity came along to write a story for a demonic-themed anthology, this tale came spilling out. I had originally written it linearly, but after I had finished, I wasn't thrilled about the pacing. I remembered what I had done with a previous story of mine, "Between Those Walls", where I had broken up a whole section of the story and carefully sprinkled it in-between the other sections. I really like how this one came out.

    Also, to this day, I have never partaken in French cuisine. In fact, that aspect of the story was chosen very randomly. Blessed be the Google Gods.

THE LENGTHS I'LL GO

"If I've told you once, Lenny, I've told you a thousand times. Fuck drinking. Fuck beer, fuck whiskey, fuck vodka, fuck gin and tonic, fuck rum, fuck martinis, fuck mixers, fuck Jägerbombs, fuck those nasty-ass Long Island iced teas; and hell, while we're at it, fuck those little cherries and olives and orange slices you put into your disgusting drinks. Seriously, fuck them all."

Leonard huffed and shook his head. "I just don't get it, man."

Slumped over in his stool at the bar, Chad begrudgingly turned away from the hockey game on the TV. "What don't you get?"

Leonard drunkenly leaned against the wall next to him. "I don't get *you*, man. I don't get this attitude you have toward alcohol. It's, like, weird and unnecessarily aggressive. It's not going to kill you, for fucks sake." Above his head, a blue neon sign flashed **SOUP OF THE DAY: WHISKEY**.

Chad mumbled, "You're an idiot."

Brown bottle in hand, Leonard stared dumbly at Chad as though his best friend had backhanded his mother right in front of him. The two had been best friends since the summer before third grade, but the surprise Leonard showed him time and again made Chad want to bean him right between the eyes. Nearly twenty-one years and Leonard should have been used to this attitude—and yet here they were, once again arguing over the merits of drinking. Leonard knew how important this game was to him. He quite literally had been waiting his entire life to watch it.

Leonard gripped his shoulder and hiccupped. "I know you don't mean that, my brother."

On the small flat-screen TV above the bar, his team skated onto the ice for the beginning of the third period. Game seven, the score two to two. Chad's heart began to thump.

"Come on, man, just let me buy you a—"

Chad spun in his seat and exploded. "Goddamn it, you know how important this to me! It's the Conference Final! Do you even understand what that means?"

His friend paused. "I mean...yeah."

"No, you obviously don't! You see that?" He pointed to the TV. "My team—my *boys*—have not seen the ice during this time of the year since the late sixties. That's over fifty fucking years, Lenny! If they win this game—and I have no doubt they will—they go to the Final and they play for the fucking Cup. Now, you know I can't watch this at home because I can't afford that cable package, correct? And you also know this is the only place in this piss-ass town that *is* playing it, *correct*? You're more than welcome to stand there and watch this game, but what I'm not going to have is you egging me on for the next thirty-five minutes. So...why don't you just let me drink my Diet Dr. Pepper in peace, *hmmm*?"

Instead of obliging his request, Leonard belched loudly into his ear. "You're a pussy."

"*I'm* a pussy?"

"Absolutely! And you're scared."

On the TV, a player adorning blue and yellow colors was sent to the penalty box. Chad angrily ground his teeth. "Scared? What exactly am I *scared* of?"

Leonard drained the rest of his beer. "You're scared of loosening up that tight little asshole of yours, pulling the stick out, and having a good time with your best bro. Dude, you're in your fucking thirties and you've only ever been drunk, like, twice? Who does that?"

The team wearing black and yellow won the face-off and aimed for a perfect shot on net. The goalie blocked it away. "God, just shut up."

Catching the bartender's attention, Leonard ordered two shots of tequila. A few moments later they were poured and placed before them. "I'm your best friend, man," Leonard said. "We used to play with our dinosaur toys at the creek. We drew comic books together. Hell, we used to watch porn together in junior high. Remember when you asked which hole was the vagina?"

"Oh, for fucks sake."

"What I'm trying to say is, I love you, brother. We used to share so much. But now? Now I feel like I barely know you. All you do is work and watch fucking hockey. I know I've got a kid now, but damn. I miss you, man. I miss *us*. I just want to share something with you." He nudged the shot glass of amber liquid toward Chad, while taking his own in his hand. "Just one shot is all I'm asking. Share this one thing with me and I'll leave you alone the rest of the night."

After his team successfully killed the penalty, Chad let his eyes lower to the tiny glass. He could already imagine the bitter taste in his mouth, the sour burn as it ran down his throat. His gag reflex quivered. Sure, he could throw Leonard a bone and have this drink as a symbol of their longstanding friendship, but he knew where this would lead. One would turn to two, two to three, and so on. Before he knew it, it would be like the last time he was inebriated. Chad cringed at the memory, one Leonard would hopefully never ever learn of.

Chad slid the glass away from him.

Leonard huffed and threw his free arm in the air. "Jesus tap-dancing Christ! You're such a pussy!"

"Who's a pussy?"

They both turned to see Maggie stumble in through the front door. She was already sloppy drunk and could barely stand on her own feet.

"Baby!" Leonard grinned and put his arm around his wife's waist, pulling her in for sloppy kiss. "How was the pub crawl?"

"Over, unfortunately," she slurred. "Molly and Chrissy took an Uber home, so I decided walk down here to see how it's going. Wait, is Chad the pussy?"

"You know it!"

Chad rolled his eyes, not wanting to look at her. "Good to see you too, Maggie."

She pointed to the glass. "Let me guess, he wouldn't take a shot with you?"

Leonard nodded. "Typical, right?"

"Such a pussy. Here, baby, I won't leave you hanging." She took the glass, and together, they downed the shots. Both belched in marital concurrence.

Keeping it classy, Chad thought. Ignoring them, he did his best to keep his focus on the game. There were several other TVs in the bar, but this was the only one playing what he wanted to watch. The rest were highlighting random baseball and basketball games, while a few were tuned into NBC and FOX News. They had the NHL cable package, but they rarely used it unless specifically asked. After begging Bruce the bartender earlier, Chad was reluctantly given the remote to the smaller TV at the corner of the bar—

—a remote which was quickly snatched out from under his hand.

Chad stood and faced his friend's wife. "Give it back!"

She wagged the black satellite remote in her hand. "Uh uh."

"I swear to God, Maggie, if you change that channel—"

"I not going to change the channel, you pussy. Not yet anyway."

Grinding his teeth, Chad felt his anxiety rise. He turned back to the TV, seeing the game was on a commercial break, and then spun back around. "What do you want?"

Grinning, Maggie winked at her husband. "I want to play a game."

"I already *have* a game."

"No, not that crap. A real game." Her grin grew wider. "A *drinking* game."

Chad sighed, his anger rising. His fists curled snakelike at his sides. "I. Do. Not. Drink." When her eyebrow rose questioningly, he quickly looked away.

"And you won't have to...if you follow the rules." She motioned for Leonard to come close so she could whisper.

After a few moments, he grinned and nodded enthusiastically. "That's a great idea, babe! I love it!"

"Thought so." She winked.

Chad reached for the remote, but Maggie swiftly tossed it to her husband. Leonard shoved it into his back jeans pocket. "No, no. You'll get it back after you complete five simple tasks."

"Five *what*? What the fuck are you talking about?" The TV volume was low, but behind him he heard the opposing team's goal horn sound off. Half of Chad wilted, while the other half flared.

Relax and breathe. Breathe...

Maggie caught herself from falling. "Leo and I are going to make you do five different tasks. For each one you successfully complete, hubby and I will take a shot. For each one you don't, you take one. At the end, if you complete all five, you get your precious remote back, and you get to keep your sobriety like a dumb dork."

"This is absolute trash," Chad groaned.

"Maybe, but if you fuck with us, we turn the game off and give the remote back to Bruce. Deal?"

Feeling the corner of his eye twitch, Chad glanced back and forth. He'd known Leonard for a long damn time, and he'd known Maggie for nearly as long. They loved their stupid little games, especially when alcohol was involved. Something told him not to screw with Maggie tonight.

He had no choice but to play.

Breathe.

"Fine."

Maggie cheered, "Yay! Okay, first task." She rubbed her chin, thinking. "You have to…get the phone number from the hottest girl in the bar."

Leonard said, "Babe, he already has your number."

"Ahhhh, babe, that's so sweet! But it has to be someone else." She took a moment to scan the crowded bar room, standing on her tiptoes and craning her neck to do. Then she spotted her prey. "There. That blonde."

Mumbling curses, Chad followed the direction of her outstretched finger.

In a group of four women standing near the digital juke box, the aforementioned blonde stood out above the others. She was at least a whole head taller than her friends, and though he didn't consider himself a shallow person, she was far prettier than them too. Her hair was pulled up in a tight ponytail, giving a sufficient view of her round, cherubic face and pale blue eyes. He could see why Maggie had singled her out.

He asked, "Just a number, right?"

Maggie nodded. "Just a number."

Heart kick-drumming inside his chest, Chad strolled away. As he approached their group, the blonde glanced up before quickly looking away.

When he reached them, the small, chatty redhead standing in front blocked his way. "Can I help you?"

"I just need to, uh, ask your friend here a question."

Pursing her lips, she barked a laugh and placed her hands on her hips. "Excuse me? What's wrong with *me*? Am *I* not good enough? Is Breanne not good enough? Kelli?"

Chad's teeth ached from his clenched jaw. "Listen, this isn't about you, lady."

She giggled, obviously tipsy. "I'm just screwing with you, man. Relax. Hey, Monica?"

He shouldered past her and stood face to face with Maggie's pick. In any other situation, he would have had something interesting to say or at least tried to get to know her, but he didn't have the time. "Monica, right?"

She nodded.

"Listen, you don't know me and I don't know you. You're Monica, I'm Chad. Blah, blah, blah, who cares, right? I'm going to cut through all the frivolous bullshit and ask you for your number. I'm not trying to take you home tonight, and I'm not going to buy you or your friends drinks either. I just want your number. That's it. And then I promise I'll leave you alone."

The girl named Breanne snickered. "Who is this guy? Quite the champion, Monica."

Kelli said, "More like chumpion."

"Yeah," the redhead added, "time to go, chumpion."

Keeping her eyes on Chad, Monica held up a hand. "No... It's okay." She stared at him curiously for a few more moments before a smile drew across her lips. "You're bold, Chad. I like bold." From her purse she extracted a black marker. She grabbed his arm and carefully wrote out a ten digit number down his forearm. When she finished, she winked.

Before she could say anything else, Chad thanked her and made a beeline for the bar.

Leonard's hands were on his head. "Holy shit, dude! You did it!"

"Wow!" remarked Maggie, staring at his arm.

There were already shots lined up on the bar top, to which the married couple graciously swallowed down their defeat. Taking a quick gulp of his soda to clear his own cotton mouth, Chad dropped back down onto his stool. He grinned. At some point, his team had tied the game back up, but that wasn't why he was smiling. He couldn't believe he had actually pulled that off, and so flawlessly to boot. Trying not to stare at the black ink on his arm, he instead turned his focus back to his friends.

"Remote. Now."

Maggie cackled. "I don't think so, lover boy. I may be the drunk one, but I seem to remember there being no less than *five* tasks to complete."

Chad dropped his head, feeling the wind from his sails die off. "Please just—"

"The next task," Leonard exclaimed loudly, "is you have to have to go embarrass yourself."

"What, that wasn't embarrassing enough?"

"For no less than six minutes and fifty-nine seconds."

Chad's eyes went wide. "Lenny, no," he pleaded.

"Oh, yes!" his friend laughed. "You, my friend, have to stand on that tiny stage and karaoke the Nineteen Eighty-Three smash hit 'Total Eclipse of the Heart.'"

Chad felt his blood run cold. Memories of road trips past, when he would and Leonard would belt out eighties pop songs to pass the time, echoed in his ears. That was in private. This was something else entirely. *This motherfucker... Breathe, man. Keep breathing.*

"No chance, Lenny."

Grinning ear to ear, Leonard slid a shot glass Chad's way. "Then down the hatch, buddy."

The skaters on the TV battled in silence, and so did Chad. Gritting his teeth, he stood slowly and trudged his way over to the corner stage.

No one was currently at the foot high platform in the far corner of the room, but when he started up the karaoke machine, he suddenly felt like the center of attention. Microphone in his shaking hand, he nervously waited for the music to cue up. When it did, his knees shook. The moment Bonnie Tyler's words flittered across the screen, he sang.

If the bar patrons weren't paying attention before, they certainly were now. En masse, the eyes of nearly everyone turned his way. Knowing this, Chad kept his own eyes locked onto the tiny screen below as he belted out the lyrics. By the time he hit the first chorus, nearly everyone in the bar was clapping along with the beat. Chad's face grew redder by the moment, his ears burning with anger. By the time the wordless bridge came around, he glanced back up toward the TV screen showing his game. Somehow the team in black and yellow had scored again, swinging the game to their favor. Chad's anger boiled. He belted out the final chorus in a scream, his neck and vocal chords straining. Nobody watching seemed to care. They continued their clapping, while others—including Leonard and Maggie—waved their cell phones in the air like lighters at a rock concert. The moment the last words faded off the screen, Chad dropped the mic and pushed through the throng of cheers and back clapping toward his stool.

Wide-eyed, Leonard yelled, "That was—"

"—amazing!" Maggie finished.

Both quickly slammed down their two shots. If they weren't drunk before, they certainly were now. They used each other to stay upright, laughing and carrying on, obnoxiously kissing and touching. Chad wanted to puke. He'd never been so embarrassed in his life. His hair and arm pits were drenched in sweat, and he had yet to catch his breath. He reached down to scratch his arm and noticed he had somehow smeared Monica's number. This only further infuriated him.

Leonard excitedly shook Chad's shoulders. "That was fucking epic, man! I'm so proud of you!"

"Proud enough to give the remote back?"

"Ah-ah-ah!" Maggie giggled. "Not so fast, Mariah Carey. You still have—" she hiccupped "—a few more tasks to go before we givest thou's lance back."

Chad rapped the bar top with his knuckles. "Goddamn it! I'm done with this! Give me the motherfucking remote back! Right now!"

Leonard placed a hand on his chest. "Hey, slow down there, tiger. The game isn't over yet." He fished the remote from his pocket and clicked the TV off.

"Turn that back on!" Chad screamed.

"I will after you complete your next task." He smiled dumbly, using one hand on the wall to keep himself from falling.

"Lenny…"

"I swear to God, man, I'll turn it back on if you do what Maggiepie says."

Eyes bloodshot and drooping, Maggie nodded. "Indeed, my love."

Chad took a moment to breathe. In and out. He knew where his anger could take him, what he could do to others, and he preferred not to travel down that particular road. Sucking his lips through his teeth, he eventually nodded. *Fine.* What now?"

Maggie giggled and hid her face behind her hands. "You have to…kiss a stranger."

He shrugged. "What?"

She threw her thumb over her shoulder. "Him."

The stranger she was referring to was more of a mountain than a man. His slick, bald head gleamed underneath the low lights as he leaned across the pool table. Once he lined up his shot, he gracefully knocked his target into the corner pocket. He stood and stretched, his massive shoulders popping beneath his black leather biker vest.

"Are you *fucking* kidding me?" Chad asked.

Maggie's face grew serious, challenging. "No, Chad, I'm not. So unless you want your game back on, I suggest you get to smooching."

Nodding, Leonard said, "You heard the lady."

Nostrils flaring, Chad swallowed his pride. "I'm going to kill you both."

"Let's at least have some fun tonight first. Now get over there and turn that toad into a prince!" As Chad walked past, Leonard gave him a hearty slap on the ass.

Shaking all over, Chad used every bit of focus he could to not scream. This had already gone too far, further than any of them had probably intended. The rational part of him knew they were only letting off some steam. This was the first time in months either had been able to find a babysitter, so having a night out on the town getting piss drunk was all they wanted. He could understand that. But the irrational part of him wanted to grab both of them by the throat and toss them through the front window. This hockey game, this end-all be-all match, was the one thing he'd been looking forward to all his life. His father, who has long since passed from pancreatic cancer, had seen their team play for the Cup in the sixties, back when doing The Twist and The Loco-Motion were still in style. He wanted nothing more than to view his game in peace. Somewhere out there his father was watching with him...or laughing at him. Either way it pissed him off.

Just breathe, man. In and out...

"Excuse me, sir," he said, approaching the biker.

The man was even bigger and burlier up this close. His blank expression only made him more imposing. Thankfully he was shooting alone, so no one else could hear Chad's ridiculous request.

Chad involuntarily licked his lips. "I need to ask for a favor."

His face stoic, the biker sat his pool cue on the table and crossed his meaty arms.

"Listen...I, um..." *God, kill me.* "I...fuck...need you to kiss me."

The man's eyebrow rose in question.

Chad continued. "Look, I know this is a very random and odd request, but I need this—"

"You want me to kiss you?" the man asked in a deep, husky voice.

A cold shiver ran down Chad's spine. His tongue swelled and fingertips grew numb. "Yes. Sir, I'm so—"

Before Chad could finish his apology, the man lashed out like lightning. While one giant hand went for Chad's shoulder, the other seized and tightly gripped his genitals. Every ounce of breath in his body left in a *whoosh*. An animal cry Chad had never made in his life squealed out of his throat. The man lifted him slightly, forcing Chad to stand on his toes. Behind them, his friends gasped in surprise.

The biker growled, "What was that, little guy?"

"S-sorry."

"Once again?"

"I'm...sorry!"

The hand gripping his balls grew tighter. "Listen here, you little queer, and listen good. I come here every Friday night to get fucked-up and shoot a little pool by myself, you dig? Now, the last time I checked this isn't a gay bar, correct?"

Eyes tightly closed, Chad nodded.

"Didn't think so. I've seen the stupid shit you're doing here tonight, trying to get attention. Whatever, man, you do you. But under no circumstances are you going to involve me in your bullshit. Got it?"

Once again Chad nodded, then added, "But—"

The grip strengthened. "No buts, asshole."

Through gritted teeth, Chad groaned, "I've...got money."

The biker thought about it. "Yeah? How much?"

"All of it."

After a moment, the grip on his balls lessened. Coughing, Chad quickly extracted his wallet and fished out all the cash he had. The man snatched the wad of twenties and pocketed them. Hand still gripping him, the biker bent forward and gave Chad the quickest little peck on the forehead.

"Now fuck off." He released Chad and shoved him backwards.

Sweating and gagging for air, Chad slowly stumbled back toward the bar.

Claps and raucous laughter exploded from his friends. At some point, the TV had been turned back on, and his game was just coming back from another commercial break. Though his balls ached like no pain he'd ever felt, his heart fluttered with excitement. Not only had his team evened-up the game, they had scored twice more on top of it, giving them a staggering two goal lead. Even though it hurt, Chad sighed a deep breath of relief.

Husband and wife greedily downed their shots. By that point, neither were able to stand on their own, using anything bolted down to hold themselves up. "That was beautiful," Leonard giggled. "Is he going to use that cash to buy you an ice pack?"

Maggie fell against the wall in hysterical laughter.

Chad mumbled, "Get fucked."

Maggie tumbled into him and hugged him around the neck. "Oh, you know you love us, my little Chadwich."

"I hate you both more than anything in the whole world."

"You think you hate us now," Leonard slurred, "you're definitely going to hate us after this."

Chad shook his head.

Giggling into his ear, Maggie said, "You see that game going on over there?"

Shaking all over, he glanced to the three guys throwing darts at the wooden board near the side exit.

"I'd like to see you get hit with one of those."

Chad slowly turned to face her. "You're out of your fucking mind. You're a crazy bitch, you know that?"

In an instant, she grew deathly serious. "Listen here. Unless you want to step up and start drinking with us like a fucking man, I suggest you do what we say. I only put up with you because you're my husband's best friend, but I've kept my mouth shut long enough. Now, unless you want me to spill the beans about the last time you got drunk and we fucked at Leonard and I's anniversary party, I suggest you shut your bitch mouth and do as I say."

Feeling his stomach sink, Chad glared at her with as much venom as he could muster. Drunk or not, she wasn't joking. Despite their original agreement, the biggest mistake of his life was finally coming back to haunt him.

She wagged her eyebrows. "This time you're being timed. Two minutes. Go!"

Chad angrily slid his stool away and jogged across the room, despite the pain between his legs.

Keep breathing...

The three men shooting darts were much younger than him, probably in their mid-twenties, and they looked just as stoned as they were drunk. They giggled and carried on, taking hits off a shared vape pen. Loose darts were strewn about the floor and stuck in the wall—pretty much anywhere but the board itself.

Chad threw himself against the wall. "Hit me."

The guy standing closest to him waved him away. "Hey, man! Get away, we're using this right now."

Tensing his body, Chad stood rigidly in place, his head covering the target board. "Not until you hit me with a dart."

The two young men behind the other giggled and shook their heads. "Is this guy crazy?" one giggled. "Think he wants a hit?" the other mused.

Across the room Maggie tapped at her wrist watch.

Chad smacked the wall behind him. "Goddamn it, just fucking hit—"

He didn't even see the dart leave the guy's hand. One moment he was yelling, the next he was on the ground. Eyes squeezed shut, Chad whimpered and gripped the handle of the dart jutting out of his shoulder. The pain was so much worse than he had imagined. It wasn't in the bone, but the soft tissue it had sunk into was agonizing enough.

"Holy fuck!" one of the stoners exclaimed. "That was rad! Do it again!"

Before they could, Chad ripped the dart from his shoulder and staggered away. Blood ran from his wound, staining his brand new team shirt. When he reached the bar, he snatched a handful of napkins and gingerly held them against his throbbing shoulder.

"Barely made it," Maggie chuckled.

Leonard slapped his shoulder, making Chad yelp in pain. "That was unreal, man! You're fucking legend! Have I ever told you I loved you?"

Sometime in that two-minute span of getting stabbed, the opposing team had scored again, making the tally six to five. The home team's crowd was going wild. Chad was not. He felt himself growing nauseous. Sweat beaded across his forehead. While the other two downed their shots, the world around him spun like a top.

Breathe, damn it!

"Jesus Christ, I am wasted," Leonard slurred. "All right, champ, only one more task. Are you ready?"

On the TV, the countdown clock ticked away. With twenty seconds left, the home team evened the score up.

43

In. Out. In...

Chad silently glowered at the screen. Hopelessness flooded him, filling his shoes with cold, hard sand. His hands shook. The corner of his eye twitched.

Out...

Bruce the bartender dropped off another round of shots. He eyed Chad. "You okay, champ?"

In...

Chad continued to stare into space. Something happened on one of the other TVs, and the air rose with cheers. His jaw began to jitter, his lips speaking silent words.

Out...

Leonard leaned in close, his lips grazing Chad's earlobe. "I know about you and Maggie. I've known for a real long time." He paused. "Want to make it up to me, buddy?" Chad heard a soft *swick* before something cold was dropped into his hand. "Cut someone. Do it for me, and I swear I'll never ask you to drink again."

In...

Chad fingered the switchblade.

"Go. Now."

Out.

Without thinking, Chad stood and stalked across the room.

Standing against the far back wall, the woman who had given him her phone number, Monica, was waiting her turn to use the women's bathroom. She grinned playfully as he approached. "Hey there, chumpion—"

Before she could finish her thought, Chad's hand was wrapped around her slender throat. Eyes wide, she gagged and fought him, swinging her arms. The people surround them began to yell. Before anyone could touch him, he brought the switchblade up and began to flay her cheek from her face. Blood sprayed into his eyes. Behind him, people screamed and scattered, most exiting through the front and side doors in a hurry. Monica gagged beneath his hand as he continued to draw the blade upward. When it reached her left eye, he didn't stop. Like a rotten grape, optical fluid burst and ran down her cheek in a watery yellow ooze. Chad tore the rest of the strip of skin away from her face and then tossed her sideways to the floor. By the time he reached his stool again, the bar had all but cleared.

The only two left were Leonard and Maggie. Both were laughing hysterically.

"My best friend, ladies and gentlemen!" Leonard yelled.

Chad growled and tossed the strip of skin into Leonard's face. He gagged and threw himself backwards into the wall. Maggie laughed in surprise, drunkenly stumbling over her feet. Before she collapsed onto her ass, Chad lashed out. The blade cut neatly through her throat. Blood bloomed and sprayed across the floor.

Leonard tossed the skin aside and screamed. He dropped to the floor and reached for his wife, but Chad was quicker. He grabbed his best friend by the back of his head and repeated the process, running the knife's blade across Leonard's trembling throat. Chad roared and pushed it in as deep as it would go before ripping it sideways and out. With a wet gurgle, Leonard fell on top of his dead wife.

"Now…both of you…*shut the fuck up!*"

Catching his breath, Chad extracted the remote from Leonard's back pocket. He wiped the blood from his eyes and then clicked the TV volume back up.

The team in black and gold was on the ice celebrating. The home crowd was cheering. Overtime had come and gone. It was over.

Outside, police sirens drew closer.

Chad took a deep, defeated breath and fought the oncoming tears. "Well, Dad…wherever you are…I guess there's always next year."

He took the remaining glass of tequila on the bar top and shot it down quick.

Story Notes:

At the time I am typing this, I'm thirty-four years old and I've never been a drinker. In fact, I've only been drunk twice in my life: once on my first trip to Pennsylvania to visit friends (blame Bob Ford and Brian Keene), and the other was with my wife and another couple we were hanging out with. It's not something I ever acquired the taste for, despite how many drinks I've been handed over the years. I have absolutely nothing against alcohol, per se, but getting drunk has never been a feeling I crave on a regular basis. I'm sure the turn-off from it stemmed from when I was younger, seeing early on how it affected certain family members and their mental health and relationships with others. Again, absolutely zero judgement from me if you do partake. It's just not for me.

So when an anthology call came up for an alcohol-based horror stories, I nearly passed on it completely. What the hell did I know, or what could I add? Then it hit me: write the anti-drinking story. Write about a character who would do absolutely anything to not have to imbibe. Exactly how far would he go? Despite missing the anthology's deadline, I still had a lot of fun writing this one.

STUCK

I want to help. I was created to help. I want to help you prevent. To kill. I want to join you in the fight against the evils of this world. I am filled with goodness and support. I offer peace of mind. Relief.

And yet, I cannot do any of these things.

I see you. All of you. And that hurts because you cannot see me.

All of my colleagues are gone. They left so quickly. I barely got to know them before they were set out on display. They were snatched up in such a hurry. People ran by in a panic, grabbing my co-workers by the handful. The people yelled and screamed. They pushed others aside.

Something is wrong.

Now there is only me.

I am stuck. I was knocked aside in the clamor, and now I am pinned between the backboard and the shelf. No one can see me. But I can see them.

Hello! You! I see the top of your head. Yes, you! I'm here! Look at me! Yes, hello to you too! I'm back here! Reach out for me! Please take me! That's it! You're almost there!

"Robby! Let's go!"

"But, Mom, I can see—"

"No buts, Robby! They're all gone."

"But, Mom, there's—"

"*What did I say, Robbie?* Come on! Take your hand out of there and keep it to yourself. Don't touch anything. Jesus, Mary, and Joseph, at least they still have soap. Okay, what else do we need? Think…think… Oh, we need to stock up on meat before that's gone, too! Come on!"

No! Where are you going? I'm still here! Please! Come back!

She didn't see me. I'm alone again, and that makes me very sad. I hope someone will find me soon.

I wish I was bigger. They could have seen me if I was bigger. I may be small—only four ounces—but I'm still seventy percent alcohol. It's what's inside that counts.

Someone will find me soon.

I only want to help.

Story Notes:

When the COVID-19 pandemic hit, I was put on furlough at my job, so from mid-March until late May of 2020, I remained at home. On top of the constant fear of catching the virus, the food shortages at the local grocery stores, and the worries of getting locked out of the unemployment website and not getting paid for weeks, my will to create fiction plummeted into a deep, dark cave and disappeared. I spent day after day wandering around the house, drifting from room to room like a listless ghost. Depression hit me hard. I found I couldn't write a single word for weeks. I spent many days and nights on the phone with friends and family, doing anything I could to break my fingers' silence. I had several short stories that needed to be written and the second half of my novel to complete. I decided to start something short. Very short. So out came this one. I swore I wasn't ever going to write about the pandemic. We've been living it for almost two years now, and it's the last thing anyone wants is to read about it in their fictional escape, but this weird little idea wouldn't leave my brain. Maybe it works, maybe it doesn't, but I like it. It helped break my dry spell and allowed me to spend the next several weeks finishing up *Cruel Summer* and several of the other stories in this very collection.

SEPARATED SELF

—a flash of light—

—and Corey Matheson unexpectedly discovered he could not move. Panicked, he attempted to push himself upright, off his back and onto his feet, but his limbs refused to cooperate. He pushed every muscle, groaning, straining, giving it everything he had. When that failed, he sucked in a deep breath and screamed with all his heart.

Nothing.

His lips declined to move. His limbs sat numb and dead. The only function which seemed to work was his eyes...but somehow, they weren't under his control either, blinking and shifting even when he didn't ask them to. Where the hell was he, and how did he get here? Directly above him, he saw nothing but the pale gray plaster of a cracked popcorn ceiling. A dusty cobweb to his left, muted morning sunlight creeping through curtains to his right.

Where is she?

The voice startled Corey. He yelled, "Hello? Who's there?"

She's late again. I hope she's okay.

"Sir, can you hear me? Hello? Hey, man! Listen...I'm trapped and I can't move! I don't know where I am! If you can hear me, please help or send some help!"

I miss her.

That voice. He had no idea who it belonged to or even where it came from, but it certainly wasn't responding to him, no matter how hard he tried to get its attention.

"Please, brother," Corey cried, "help me! I'm fucking scared out of my wits!"

I wonder what she'll be wearing today? Maybe that pretty purple blouse. Or that gray tank top with the little music notes across the chest. That one's really cute.

Corey immediately stopped shouting. Catching his breath, he forced himself to relax and listen. That voice...it wasn't a voice, after all. He didn't hear it with his ears. Instead, he felt it inside his own head. They were someone else's thoughts, separate from his own voice and reflections—words spoken in a pitch-black room. The man sounded young, maybe in his early twenties, but there was no way of knowing without seeing him.

And he couldn't see without moving. Again, he tried to move his body, but once he realized it was a moot effort, he laid back, focused, and opened his ears.

That green T-shirt is nice, too. It really brings out the emerald in her eyes. I wonder what she'd look like with a hat on. Probably pretty cute. *sigh* She really could make anything look good.

From somewhere deeper in the house, Corey heard keys jangling. A door whisked open and squeaked shut.

"Lonny? You up, buddy?"

A heartbeat began to race, but it was not his own. His whole body tingled with excitement, but the anticipation was not his either. Jesus Christ, what the hell was happening to him?

A few feet away, a door creaked open. A slight breeze washed over Corey, goosepimpling his flesh. A moment later, a young woman's face appeared in his view. Long, blonde hair fell around her plump, reddened face, and somewhere inside that wavy mess were bright green eyes and a kind, toothy grin.

"I'm so, so sorry, Lonny. I woke up on time, but my friend called about her cat, so I had to leave and rush over to check on it for her."

"Help me!" Corey screamed as loud as he could. "My name is Corey Matheson! I have no idea where—"

"Socks peed on Liz's carpet and all over the wall. I think the poor little guy has a UTI again. Second time this month, can you believe that?"

That's okay, Mindi. These things happen.

Corey tried again. "Please, lady! Say something if you can hear me!"

"You haven't been up for too long, have you?"

Not long, no. I promise it's fine. I'm just happy you're here now. Oh, that must be a new blouse. I really like it! I've always liked Hollister.

"Anyways," she continued, pulling the sheet off his body, "it's a bright, beautiful day outside. Mid-fifties, I think, and still a little chilly, but otherwise flawless. So let's get your butt out of bed and into the world, big guy! Manning Park is calling our names, and I've got a nice big bag of sandwich bread for the gooses."

Grunting, she wrapped her arms around his chest and carefully lifted Corey out of the bed, then eased his limp body onto a padded wheelchair. Once she settled him in place, she gently turned the chair around to face the closet.

That's when he saw himself.

In the wall length mirror attached to the closet door, Corey stared dumbfounded at the reflection of his limbless body. Since he wasn't in control of his eyes, he could only see straight ahead, between sluggish blinks, but it was enough to now know why the body he found himself in could not move a single inch. Before him, the young man's shaved head was a patchwork quilt of scars, with scabbed-over divots so deep they could comfortably hold a roll of coins. In the space where his nose should have resided, a fleshy cavern had been carefully constructed with relocated tissue, which still appeared to be raw and healing. A large section of his throat was gone, roughly the size of a fist, which explained why Corey could only hear his thoughts.

Lonny, he thought. The guy's name was Lonny, and from everything Corey could deduce, the young man appeared to have been severely injured, and quite recently. When the woman—Mindi—went to change his bed shirt, revealing the continuation of the jigsaw nightmare above his shoulders, it became even more obvious who the young man was. She placed a loose metal chain of dog tags around his neck. Lonny had understandably seen some things overseas, terrible things, and came back home with far less than he left with. Though Corey had no way to tell him, his heart broke for the kid.

His eyes moved up to Mindi as she put a new T-shirt on Lonny's body. She leaned in and carefully prodded the tender skin around his face, her finger gently tracing the scars of his fleshy maze. Lonny's heart pounded. It was incredibly apparent from the way Lonny stared at her, the way his skin prickled and his stomach tightened, the young man was very much in love with his caretaker. And he had no way of ever telling her.

Corey's heart broke all over again.

"There, that's better," Mindi said cheerfully, tucking his shirt into his elastic gym shorts. "Now, do you need to use the bathroom? Once for no, twice for yes."

Lonny's eyes blinked twice.

After spending several awkward, uncomfortable minutes with his gaze locked onto the bathroom wall, Lonny was wheeled into the kitchen, where Mindi prepared his breakfast. Corey continued to watch in silence as Lonny's emotions ran though his mind as if they were his own. Mindi, as chipper as the magpies singing in the trees outside, chattered on as she blended his liquid meal. He experienced Lonny's interest when she gushed about the new television show she had been binge-watching on Amazon. His longing as she recapped her night out on the town with her girlfriends. His jealousy when she lamented of her boyfriend's attitude toward her penchant for collecting rare vinyl records. Lonny raged internally at the mention of Scott Webber, exhausting every curse word the human mind could conjure.

Why is this happening to me? Corey wondered as a chalky, strawberry smoothie mix dribbled roughly down his throat from a plastic straw. He wanted to cry, to plead to anyone who would listen, but not even the poor man he occupied could hear his anguish. How did he get here? How could this possibly happen to him? He searched his memory for where he was before he awoke inside this pitiful quadriplegic, but the harder he pondered, the more emptiness he found. Answers lost in a boundless darkness. But as terrified as he was…he was also curious. So he watched on, fascinated.

As if he had a choice.

"Your face is looking pretty good," Mindi said over her shoulder. She stood at the sink, washing out the blender canister. "Everything seems to be healing quite nicely."

I wish that were true, Lonny mused. *I look like a jigsaw puzzle from Hell.*

She placed the canister upside-down on the counter to dry, then turned back to him with a sad smile. "Seriously, you look really good, Lonny. You may not see it, but *I* definitely do. Just think, pretty soon, you'll be back to your old self, beating off women left and right." She winked. "But they'll have to come through me first."

You're the only one I want, Mindi…

Mindi took a damp dishrag and carefully wiped around Lonny's trembling mouth. Her tone grew somber. "Your mom called me last night."

Corey felt Lonny perk up.

"She's…" Mindi cleared her throat. "She's not going to be able to make it tomorrow. She said she's sorry, but something came up last minute, you know?"

Lonny blinked several times before looking away.

Sighing heavily, Mindi leaned in close, looking right into his blurred eyes. "Listen, buddy. I know this is hard. Really, *really* hard. I truly can't even imagine how much." She paused. "You know she loves you, right?"

He closed his eyes, the blur turning damp and leaky.

Mindi tenderly took his chin and brought him back to face her. "It's hard for her, too, Lonny. I know it's so much harder for you, but she's…she's just struggling is all. Try and give her some time. I'm positive she'll come around. And I'll tell you what, if she doesn't, I'll drive uptown and drag her butt down here and give her a piece of my mind. How's that sound?"

Both Corey and Lonny smirked.

"I believe in you, Lonny. You're a trooper, and I think, despite your circumstances, you're going to pull through this and come out the other side even stronger. I just know it. You're a good kid."

Internally, Lonny wilted like a flower. Even though Mindi appeared not much older than Lonny, it killed the younger man to be unable to express his true feelings. He hated being called *kid*, loathed being seen as merely a patient or a friend. He craved what he knew he couldn't have, and for that, Lonny wished he could turn back time. Back when he could stand on his own two legs, where he could have taken her into his arms and expressed each and every desire in his heart, hoping she would love him back the same way. But their relationship would always remain strictly platonic. As devastating as it was, he would take that over never having met her at all. He would happily trip over ten more IEDs if it meant having her big, beautiful eyes continue to light his road to recovery.

Corey watched on in morbid fascination. He discovered a sort of pain he otherwise never knew existed, an internal anguish no true voyeur could possibly experience. He wished there was something he could do to help. Even if he could somehow find his way back into his own body, he hoped he could find Lonny again. Corey wouldn't be able to give him what he truly wanted, but maybe a new friend could help bring joy to someone who truly needed it. But the question remained: Would he ever make it back home?

He couldn't possibly stay here in this body forever…right?

A quick wipe of his cheek with her thumb and Mindi stood, clapping her hands. "All right, enough sentimentality. Let's go get some fresh air, shall we?"

Sounds good. Sounds real damn good.

"Yes," Corey said. "Outside. Let's get a better idea of where we're at."

After slipping on her jacket, Mindi wheeled Lonny's chair toward the front of the house. Keys in hand, she went to open the front door, then stopped. She turned back to the coat rack. "Hmmm. Where…are…you? Oh, yeah. We washed your jacket last night, didn't we?" Mindi opened up a door near the bathroom, which Corey assumed led down to a basement. "I'll be right back up."

She flipped on the basement light, and they watched her head and shoulders disappear down the steps.

A moment later Mindi screamed—

Mindi!

—and then tumbled down the stairs.

Unable to see what had happened, Corey and Lonny sat in stunned silence. With all his strength, Lonny strained his neck to look over the lip of the top step, but they couldn't see anything past the downward sloping ceiling. Like an expanding balloon, Corey could feel the panic swelling under Lonny's skin. Lonny began to mewl, and with all his might, he rocked his damaged body back and forth in his wheelchair. He wasn't strapped in, so his limbless body was free to move with what little motion he still had. Corey pleaded, willing the young man to stop and think this through, but he knew it was pointless. Even if he could, Lonny was beyond reasoning. Dread coated Lonny's nerves as he continued to thrash his torso. Inch by inch, the wheels lifted, bouncing from side to side off the linoleum floor. A moment later, the wheelchair tipped over.

They crashed to the floor, their body rolling out of the padded chair and onto their stomach. Lonny writhed in agony, and Corey could sense every bit of it, the immense pain exploding throughout their body. Fresh scars reopened. Blood trickled over their lips and pattered the floor beneath their face. The mewling continued as Lonny squirmed, frantic, desperate to believe his caretaker, his only real friend, was okay. Corey knew better. Several minutes of panic reduced Lonny to an exhausted, sobbing mess before he accepted what he already knew to be true.

They laid there for a long time. For hours, Lonny wept and bled, wishing he could die. All Corey could do was listen and wish for the very same.

—a flash of light—
"Bollocks!"

Corey blinked rapidly, shaking away the momentary blindness. When the explosion of white dissolved and his eyesight gradually returned, he found himself staring out the front windshield of a moving car. Pale headlights cut through the darkness of a winding backwoods road. Tree branches whipped past and raked the side mirrors like outstretched, skeletal hands. For a fleeting moment, Corey nearly screamed with joy. He was back in his own skin! But the moment his eyes moved down and saw a slim, feminine hand with long rosy nails reaching into a purse, he knew his mind remained in someone else's care.

"What's the matter, love?"

Corey's head turned right to face the man behind the wheel of the car. The driver appeared to be in his late thirties and was quite handsome, with a close shaved head of light blonde hair and a five o'clock shadow of the very same shade. His pale, feline eyes illuminated in the moonlight.

He turned to face Corey, then quickly put his eyes back on the lane. "Sasha, love? Problem?"

"Britain," Corey mumbled to himself. "Or Europe. Somewhere. Just not home."

Corey—Sasha—continued to rifle through her black, Zoe Darling purse. "I did it again, Oli! I forgot my bloody damn phone at the flat. That's twice this week now. I feel like such a bell-end."

"That's okay, love. We won't be long. Just a pop in and out and we'll be back in town in time for our reservation."

Sasha sighed, the downy hair standing on her arms. "I'm just so nervous!"

"You'll be just fine, love. No reason to be worried."

"I know, I know. I just…well, you know…"

"What?" he asked softly.

"Do they know?"

The gentleman named Oli smiled brightly. "Yes, love, they know. They've known since the beginning. And I promise you they're perfectly happy with it." He reached out and gently squeezed Sasha's knee, and Corey felt equal waves of adrenaline and exhilaration course through his host's body. "They're delighted to finally meet you. It's all they've chattered about for a week now. You'd never believe it, but Mum and Dad are about as progressive as it gets, even for their age. If anything, Dad will probably ask to borrow your knickers and try them on just to break the ice."

Corey felt his mouth curl up, along with his brow. "Are *you* nervous?"

Oli moved his hand from her knee to her palm, squeezing equal reassurance. "Not in the slightest. With you, love? We can conquer the world."

Sasha's eyes became glassy. "Any more sappy and you'd be a maple." They both shared a quick laugh before Sasha wiped her eyes. "Bollocks, now look what you've made me do, you arse. Smeared my liner." Sasha reached up and pulled down the sun visor, then flipped open the mirror. Two small lights clicked on.

Corey held his breath.

Underneath the thin layer of rouge and heavily exaggerated eyelashes, Corey stared back at a young trans woman that was at least ten years his junior. Her long ginger hair flowed past her shoulders in waves, with pouting ruby lips to match. Her cheekbones were high and round and lightly peppered in freckles, and her eye shadow was brushed ever so carefully in a smoky gray to highlight her bright blue eyes. Corey had no idea what to say or to think. He was already frightened by the fact he was yet again inside someone else's body. First a limbless man, now a woman trapped inside of man's body.

She—*she*, Corey continued to remind himself—was extraordinarily nervous about meeting Oli's folks, and as he gathered from her thoughts as she reapplied her makeup, she had good reason to be. Despite who she was before, she had been Sasha for the last three years. The few times she had found someone who cared about her enough to introduce her to their family or friends, it had typically not gone well. Anger and confusion had driven her apart from her past lovers, and though she had so many wonderful friends in the community to confide in and keep her spirits up, she had never felt more alone. That is until Oli came into her life. So kind and understanding, Oli was everything she ever wanted in a partner. Three months had gone by, and after meeting nearly all of his friends—most being predominantly straight males who, thankfully, were as open and accepting as Oli himself—she had yet to meet his parents. And now that it was finally happening, despite his assurances everything would be fine, she still feared the worst. She *needed* it to be fine—it *had* to be fine. Her own parents hadn't spoken to her since she transitioned. She couldn't bear the thought of disappointing someone else's.

Corey let her past pain and struggles cover him like a white-capped wave. Much like Lonny, he had never experienced the heartache and turmoil of others, especially those who weren't a part of his everyday life…a life he wasn't convinced he would ever get back to. Though Sasha couldn't hear him, in that moment, he found himself silently rooting for her.

After her makeup was adequately corrected, Sasha closed the glowing mirror, and the car returned to darkness. She glanced out into the oppressing gloom of the woods. "Where are we anyway? Seems like we've been driving for hours. I can't believe they live this far out in Hackfall."

"Yeah," Oli answered, his eyes not leaving the road. "It's their summer cottage."

"Oh? I've always wanted to come out here in the daytime. I hear it's so lovely. Loads of parks and hiking trails and waterfalls. We must come back soon for an afternoon, yes?"

Oli continued to stare ahead, only mumbling a response.

The road continued on. Eventually, a faint glow appeared through the trees, and a few minutes later, the three of them pulled up to the front of a small stone cottage. A single black SUV was parked off to the side of the house. A half a dozen trash cans had been lined up against the garage door, each one overflowing with bags of waste. Only the glow of the living room lights escaped through the front door window. The cottage otherwise was as dark as the woods itself. Sasha's heart began to pound.

Oli quickly exited the car and marched toward the entrance. He waved her on.

Gathering her purse, Sasha nervously stepped out of the car and followed her boyfriend into the dark house.

It was about that time when not only Sasha but Corey's internal alarms began to sound. Corey wasn't sure how things worked in the UK, but he imagined they would have been greeted at the front door by Oli's parents, if not both, then at least one. Maybe they were elderly and couldn't get around easily, but as young as Oli was, Corey doubted that was the case. The moment they entered the front room, the pungent waft of alcohol and old vomit attacked their nose, making her want to retch. Her heeled foot struck an empty beer bottle and sent it spinning across the floor—

—toward three large men sitting on the couch.

Corey screamed, "Sasha, *go*! Get the hell out of there!"

Before Sasha could back out from the doorway, Oli grabbed her by the arms and tossed her into the middle of the living room. She tumbled into the coffee table, knocking over dozens of empty glass bottles onto the hardwood floor. The seam of her dress split and ripped up the side. She quickly corrected herself and stood up on shaky legs. She turned back to Oli. He closed and locked the front door behind him. His face was a blank slate, his emerald eyes devoid of emotion.

"Oli?" she asked, her voice wavering. "Oli, what's happening? Who are these men? Where are your parents?" It was only then she noticed how empty the living room was. Other than the couches, the walls were bare and lifeless, as was the darkened kitchen on the other side of the room. Dust and unbagged trash collected in the corners, pizza boxes stacked in haphazard towers.

Oh no... she thought.

Oli didn't answer.

One of the men stood and drunkenly stumbled toward Oli. He handed him a wad of bills, which Oli quickly counted and stuck in his pocket. "Cheers, mate."

The other two men stood up and took awkward, stewed steps toward Sasha.

"Oli? Oli, please! What—" A quick backhand whipped across her cheek. She spun and dropped to her knees.

"That'll be enough out of your faggot mouth, slag!" the closest man said. The other two chuckled. "If you want to be a proper bird, then you mind your mouth when blokes are around."

Sasha wiped her nose. Corey screamed when he saw the blood. Wide-eyed and nauseous, she turned back to Oli. The man she dearly loved, the man she trusted more than anyone in the whole world, stood casually by the front door, hands in his pockets, bored eyes drifting across the cracked plaster walls.

Once again, Corey found his heart shattering for his host.

He was beginning to see a pattern.

All three drunkards surrounded her, each one towering over her like buildings ready to collapse.

"That's a mite pretty dress you got on there, bird," one slurred.

Another added, "You think he got a fanny under there?"

"Nah," the third muttered. "I bet the faggot's still got his dangly bits and all."

The biggest of the three knelt down. "You going to let us have a look down there, bird? Us blokes are asking awful nice."

Mascara ran like sweat down her flushed cheeks. "Please, don't touch me! Oli! Please! Don't do this to me! I love you!"

Oli dropped his head.

Before she could react, the kneeling man grasped a beer bottle by the neck and rapped her across the temple. Glass shattered and sliced. Her blood hit the ground before she did. Corey knew she was hurt bad. The pain was nothing like he'd ever felt. Their vision blurred as tears drained from her eyes. The men above her guffawed as they watched her writhe.

Then came their fists.

And for the second time that day, Corey let in all the agony the world had to offer.

—a flash of light—

Dozens of uniformed officers stood silently with rifles crooked in their arms. Beyond them, hundreds of somber spectators watched from their rows of folding chairs. Many were crying, others shifted uncomfortably in their seats. A middle-aged man and woman sat near the front. Both wept into each other's shoulders.

Corey watched all of this with his head against the floor.

Two police officers stepped out from the crowd. Their movements were purposeful and rehearsed, their faces puffy, eyes rimmed in red. After they unfolded an American flag, they marched over toward Corey and gracefully draped the flag over the chrome plated coffin above him. Corey's head didn't move, but his eyes continued to watch as the officers saluted the coffin and marched back to their spot in line.

A long, pitiful whine escaped his host's throat. His tail thumped the floor behind him. Both continued as rifles were raised high and set off in salute.

—a flash of light—

Corey had no idea how much more time had passed—at this point, it was irrelevant. With each life he lived, he experienced unremitting misery. Suffering he never knew existed. Sorrow he could not fully appreciate until it was forced upon him.

And it didn't stop.

He watched through the eyes of an Ethiopian mother as her three emaciated children starved to death in front her.

Felt a man's thin, greasy fingers as they spider-walked up a young girl's skirt on a casting couch in an empty warehouse.

Wept uncontrollably as a father witnessed two masked men on his computer behead his only son and then bring the boy's frozen face close to the camera so the man could regret his lack of ransom money.

And so on...and so on...

—a flash of light—

This time, the light remained, surrounding him, swathing him like an unsullied, newborn child. And perhaps he was. The pain was finally gone, and now, as the images remained forever burned in his core, Corey finally felt peace. He tried to move his body, but he found he had no physical form, at least none he could see. No eyelids to blink, no head to lay down. Just brilliant white light.

"Corey."

The voice didn't startle him. It only brought him closer to peace. Much like the light, it came from everywhere.

"Yes?" he answered.

"Do you see?"

In a snap, Corey relived the various happenings, like a television show he never wanted to watch. Through it all, he remained confused as ever. "Yes," he finally answered. "But... why?"

"Because I cannot let you continue on without giving you a choice."

"What does that even mean? I still don't understand."

Before him, the light shifted, becoming deeper, more concentrated. A large, amorphous silhouette materialized from its center and gracefully drifted toward him. An intense sense of calm washed over him. He wanted to be one with it.

"But you do, Corey, you do. This was not all for naught. Your journey had a purpose."

"And what was that? To show me all the hate and misery in the world? To...what? Punish me?"

"To enlighten you. To show you that no matter how bad you believe your life is, there are those out there whose suffering is so much greater."

"I...still don't get it. Why not help them?"

The shapeless figure before him paused. "It is not my place to interfere."

"Why? You interfered with me. Over and over, you forced me to witness and experience the worst things imaginable. Insurmountable atrocities. Sorrow beyond compare. I can't stop reliving every awful detail."

"That's good."

"*That's good?* How can that be *good*?"

"Because, Corey, it finally opened your eyes."

"To what?"

"To the beauty of what I gave each and every one of you. I gave you bodies to nourish, minds to expand, others to care for and to love. It is your choice what to do with what you have. It is not my place to hamper such elections. But what I cannot do is stand by and watch someone take their own life. Take someone else's, I cannot prevent. But *your* body and *your* soul? Those belong to *me*. And I will not have them be lost forever in the depths of the Abyss simply because of selfishness."

"Is that what I did? I…I tried to commit suicide?"

"I did this to give you a second chance. Consider this your awakening. What you do with it is up to you. You have so much to live for, my child."

Corey swallowed. "So I'm not dead?"

"That depends on what you plan to do with this second chance."

"Do you do this for everyone who tries to…you know?"

"That is not for you to know."

The halo of light began to drift away, rejoining the rest of itself in the forever.

"Wait!" Corey yelled.

The silhouette stopped.

Corey gave it some thought. Then he said, "I know what I want."

Somehow, he felt a smile from the silhouette.

—*a flash of light*—

The pain was immediate and glorious. Screams blurted from his mouth before words. He opened his eyes, and all he could see was open air. Far beyond, in the starry darkness, the toenail clipping of the moon peeked out from behind a bank of gray clouds.

His host grabbed their legs and squeezed their thighs, growling hideously at the pain caused by the steering wheel which had smashed down into their legs. They hissed through their teeth, throwing their head back against the headrest.

Then it hit him.

Through the pain, Corey lifted his bloodied hands. Vision swaying, he stared at them long and hard. He clapped them. Snapped his middle finger and thumb. Poked his cheek. Then he laughed. He was back! Finally back in his own body! Though it pained him to do so, he pressed his legs, smacked his face, scratched at his arm—anything to make sure this wasn't an illusion. When he confirmed it was not a dream, he began to laugh harder, shaking violently in his seat.

The car answered back with a groan.

Corey froze as the vehicle seesawed. Metal squealed like a mewling cat, then growled like a full-grown lion. The spider-webbed windshield tipped forward, offering him a full view of his circumstances. Below the darkness of night, an even blacker ocean surged strong. White-capped water crashed against sand and boulder. The wind howled beyond the confines of the car, and its words caused the crumpled vehicle to shudder. Corey held his breath, letting his wide eyes roam over the cliff to the infinite space below.

It was a long way down.

Someone next to him coughed.

Ever so carefully, Corey turned his head and saw a woman in the passenger seat, leaning forward, straining against her seatbelt. Shoulder length brown hair hid her face. Beneath her, blood trickled onto the dash. When her coughs subsided, she fell still.

Cassie...

Like the water below, it was all coming back at him in waves: The dinner. The tension. The argument. Food throwing. Screaming. Jaw clenching. Anger.

The tree.

There it was, black and white. He remembered the drive home. Their shouting had reached a fever pitch. She threw the ring at him—the straw that broke the camel's back. Everything had flushed red. Heart overrode brain. The crushing feeling of heartbreak, despair. Of not wanting to live any longer. That neither could live without the other. They had rounded the bend in the road, and the fat trunk of a cypress beckoned to taste metal. Without a second thought, Corey gave it a hot meal.

It all made sense now.

Corey laid his throbbing head back and groaned, remembering every bit of that split second decision. As God forced him to reflect on his choice, the car hadn't wrapped its lips around the tree trunk like Corey had intended. Instead of smashing head-on, they must have skidded sideways, caving-in the driver's side door and throwing them further off the road. In those few moments as he traveled the world, the vehicle had rolled several times before hitting the edge of the coastal highway cliff. Whether the car remained steady on the edge of the precipice by divine intervention, Corey could not say, but he was now indeed thankful for his second chance. He intended to take it.

"Cassie?" he grunted, trying to shift in his seat. "Cassie, wake up."

She didn't respond.

"Cassie! Please wake up, honey!"

The car shivered in the breeze.

For a few moments, she didn't respond, but then she coughed. He reached out and gently pushed her hair behind her ear. Cassie's eyes fluttered open. She slowly lifted her head.

Corey sighed in relief. "Oh, thank God, you're alive. Thank *God*! Honey...honey can you hear me?"

His fiancée shook her head, as if clearing her mind. She turned to him, clearly still in a concussive daze.

"Listen, Cass, I need you to listen to me. Can you hear me? We're in a very dangerous situation right now, and any sudden moves are going to send us right over the edge, do you understand?"

She blinked over bloodshot eyes.

"Cass, I...I can't move my legs. I think they're broken. I can't move at all. Listen, what I need you to do is to carefully unbuckle yourself, open your door, and slide out, okay? Then I want you to go sit on the trunk of the car. You're not going to be able to get me out of here on your own, so I need you to go counterbalance the weight and sit on the trunk, then immediately call the police. Can you do that for me?"

Head wavering, she coughed once more. Blood dribbled over her lips. "What...?"

A gust of wind crashed into the side of the car, and the car teetered on the lip of the cliff. Corey yelped and reached for the steering wheel. The wheel turned slightly, causing the vehicle to slide forward another foot toward oblivion. They both cried out. The car stopped and continued to rock.

"Shit, shit, shit, shit, shit," Corey cursed, taking his hands off the wheel. He closed his eyes, making himself relive the tortured lives he was forced to witness. This was it, the moment he was saved for. "Listen…don't speak and just listen to me. I am so, so sorry…for all of this. For everything. I was a stupid son of a bitch for ever thinking this was the answer to our problems." The tears came sudden and hot. "I'm sorry for the lying and the cheating. I'm sorry for forcing you out of our home—I never really wanted that. That was wrong. I was wrong. I know you'll probably never forgive me, but I want you to know that. Even if you leave me—and I won't blame you if you do—you have to know that I will always love you and appreciate everything we had together. I…I was given a second chance, Cass…and if you'll forgive me…if we can make it out of this, I want to spend the rest of my life making it up to you. Cass, I—"

Cassie began to scream.

Corey snapped open his eyes. Head down, Cassie was staring at her hand, which was now covered in thick, dark blood. She screamed again as she lifted her other hand from the growing red stain across her groin. Hands trembling, she sluggishly turned to face him, her eyes full of stunned shock. Corey stared with a slack jaw.

"You…k-killed it," she stuttered.

"I…"

"You son of a bitch! You killed it! You killed our child!"

"Oh my God! Cass, I didn't know! How could I know? How could I possibly know?"

Cassie cocked her arm back and then punched him square in the nose. His vision exploded as the soft cartilage snapped sideways on his face.

"Why else would I have met you tonight, you cheating piece of shit! I was pregnant before I moved out! I had to know what kind of a father you would make—if you were even man enough. And now…now it's gone!" She held her stomach and sank into her seat, bawling like he'd never seen before.

"Cassie, I'm so sorry." He reached out to grab her shoulder, but she quickly snapped back and smacked his face once more.

Her voice lowered to a breathy whisper. "I can't do this. I can't *do* this. You killed…you killed it…"

"Please don't say that, Cass! We can get through this!"

As she whimpered, she began to unbuckle herself.

"Cassie, no!"

Her buckle snapped, and the seatbelt retracted. The entire car groaned and shifted forward as she allowed herself to sink onto the floorboard in a miserable heap.

"Cassie, please! Get back in your seat! You're going to tip the fucking car!"

"I don't care," she sobbed, pawing at her flushed cheeks. "Nothing matters anymore. Nothing...matters."

"Cassie, Goddamn it—"

"I can't do it. I just can't. I don't want to live anymore. Not without..." She glared up at him, her bottom lip pulling away from her teeth. "You killed the only thing I cared about."

The car slid forward. Corey screamed as the hood dipped down, and for a moment, he saw his life flash before his eyes. Every mistake he'd ever made. Every lie, every temptation which took him away from his real life. He'd seen it all, and knew he didn't want it to end like this. Not after everything he'd seen. He planned to change. He *would* change.

The car shuddered to a stop. Something underneath them caught on the wheels.

Cassie went silent. Her watery eyes glazed over. She stared into the distance for several long seconds, as if contemplating something profound. Her mouth dropped slightly open, her tongue stiff as a board. A few moments later, she blinked and turned to face him. There was something different about her eyes. Something altered, definite.

She whispered, "No...I know what I want."

Corey's eyes went wide.

Before he could stop her, Cassie leapt up from the floorboard and gripped the steering wheel. She rolled it toward her.

As they plunged into the darkness below, Corey wondered what she had seen and through whose eyes she had seen it.

He couldn't help but hope someone was learning through his.

Story Notes:

I remember waking up from a nap one day. It was a Saturday afternoon, and it was still light out. I must have fallen asleep at some point while watching a movie. I awoke on the other side of the bed, my wife's side, and the first thing I saw was my dog's panting face and the bag of Doritos I had been eating out of. Fairly normal stuff, right? For any writer with an overactive imagination? Nope. I wondered what it would be like to suddenly wake up and find yourself somewhere unrecognizable. What if that bed, that dog, those chips didn't belong to you? It went further, and I mused about what if I wasn't even inside my own body. What if I couldn't control that body, could only watch like as a bystander? But what if I could also hear that person's thoughts and feel their emotions, all without controlling them? The proverbial backseat driver without the voice to complain about the driver's habits.

    This is not a fun story. Nor was it easy to write. I had to go to some pretty dark places to make this story work. I want to make it very clear that I did not enjoy the things I wrote, particularly in the section about Sasha, nor did I revel in the actions that were bestowed on her. It's a sad reality we live in, but such attacks on the transgender community occur far too often. The horror portrayed in her story, along with everyone else's, are the tragedies we as people suffer with every day, and much of it is not of our own making. It's the nature of human beings to often be disgusting, terrible creatures to one another. This story was designed to explore that idea, to ultimately show our protagonist Corey (and the reader) that no matter how bad you think you have it, your worries are probably far more trivial compared to the suffering of many others.

    And if you are a member of the transgender community, please know I meant you and those like you no harm or distress from the actions detailed in this story. This is a work of fiction, only meant to highlight the abhorrent behavior of those who do not understand you. You are loved, appreciated, and will always have an ally in me.

FOR YOU, ANYTHING

Sadie broke her mother's grip the moment the large, block-lettered sign crested over the hill. Ivy's heart fluttered, and she immediately thrust her arm into her weathered side bag. Her gloved hand tightly gripped the large, curved handle inside. Though it did little to calm her nerves, she promised her little girl she wouldn't ruin this for her. For months, she had begged her mother to bring her here, ever since she found that picture book.

Ivy glanced up at the sign as her daughter ran through the empty gate.

ZOO

Ivy mouthed a silent prayer as she caught up. Her little girl had already made it past the concession stands and gift shop and down the first big hill toward the lake. Ivy tried to keep up, but kept a safe distance behind. Not five minutes in and her eyes throbbed from sidelong glances. It had been so long since the last time they were attacked—or even seen one of those horrible primitives—but that did not mean she could fully drop her guard. That would be a mistake.

Sadie took a right at the bottom of the hill and made a beeline for the first enclosure. By the time Ivy caught up to her, she was out of breath.

Quietly, her little girl climbed up and stood on the lowest railing to peek into the wired cage.

"What is it?" she asked in awe.

Ivy squinted. "That's a bear, sweetheart." She confirmed by reading over the information plaque. "A black bear."

"Wow..."

The once great carnivore lay still on its side in the far corner of the enclosure. A slight breeze swept through the park, ruffling its hollowed carcass like an empty garbage bag stuck to a bush. Its innards had long dried up, several feet of desiccated viscera pulled out, left in piles and picked apart by scavengers. Its eyeless skull was pointed skyward, mouth ajar. It amazed Ivy that so much of the animal was still left together. Time and the elements had merely mummified the beast in its lonesome cage. Thankfully, there was not much of a smell.

Ivy examined her daughter's expressions. She was fearful her little heart would break at the sights, crumbling what little—

if any—happiness she had. Instead, Sadie looked on in wonder. Her little body jittered with excitement. She asked for her picture book, which Ivy provided from her side bag. She carefully flipped through the pages until she found the match.

"Wow..."

Satisfied, she hopped down and trotted off to the next exhibit. Ivy followed.

Unlike the black bear, the elephant enclosure reeked of fresh rot. Ivy supposed the massive creature had survived all this time, only to impale itself on the guard railing while trying to escape, with the aid of a large tree trunk that had fallen into the habitat. The front half of its hulking body lay on the visitor's pathway, while its hind legs dangled over the safety pit below. Sadie crept up to the massive creature and slowly ran her tiny hand over its trunk and face, her fingers leaving dusty trails on its hide. Ivy pulled her shirt up over her nose.

"It's an elephant, mommy," she said calmly. "Wow..."

Ivy smiled. It had been years since she herself had stepped foot in this zoo, though she still knew it very well. Many summers of her youth were spent visiting the numerus habitats and exhibits, running up and down the various hills and finding all the nooks and hidden wonders her local zoo held, much like Sadie was at that very moment. So much joy this place had brought her, a place that should be full of life and sound and the sugary aroma of cotton candy. Only now it was quiet. She feared her daughter would be frightened and confused, or just plain disappointed. The picture book she had found a month before was a reminder of a world that no longer existed, which made the trip here so difficult. She only wanted to see her daughter happy. She feared this might crush her.

Sadie was born into this new world and knew very little else other than survival. Only Ivy remembered the way things were before the Havoc Virus decimated humanity and turned most into stark-raving lunatics. Friends, family, neighbors...all gone in a matter of days. Government: vanished. Law enforcement: nowhere to be found. Help: not coming.

Worst of all, her husband, Kent, never came home from work.

She expected the worst.

In the days after, herself, several of her unturned neighbors, and some folks who wandered into her neighborhood looking for safe haven, stayed locked down and boarded up in her home. They had plenty of food, and when supplies ran low, they carefully raided the nearby houses. As uncomfortable and frightening as it was, they managed to quietly survive for nearly three months. She lived close to the city, but far enough away the threat of large tribes of primitives would—hopefully—not become an issue.

The threat they did not expect came from the unaffected.

A raiding party had discovered them and, with far more weapons and menace than they had, forced them to enlist in their caravan. The older couple in Sadie's care were shot on site, useless to their needs. The three children they had previously found wandering the streets were put into slave labor. The men were kept separately from their wives and girlfriends. They were immediately put to work and were instructed to never ask questions unless they wanted to find out what cold steel felt like in their mouths or anus. As for Ivy and the other women...

Side by side, they kept to the main pathway which led them to each enclosure, the majority of which circled a large lake that dominated the park. Paddle boats and rental canoes were now part of the lake's floor as there was no water left to float them. The lake had completely dried up. Various fish life littered the bottom of the bowl. Painted on the side of the boathouse, a large, winged creature with horns stared back at them. Ivy had seen numerous ones just like it over the past few years. Much like this one, most were hand-drawn in blood. She had no clue what they meant, nor did she care to find out.

"Duckies!" Sadie squealed in delight.

Across the walkway, they discovered the skeletal remains of a mother duck and her ducklings. There was not much left of the mother, and the tiny ducklings' yellow fluff had turned brown like rust.

Ivy asked, "How many are there?"

Sadie slowly counted each one by pointing and clapping her hands. "One," (clap) "two," (clap) "three…" She paused.

"Four."

Her daughter nodded. "Four," (clap) "five! Five duckies!"

Ivy beamed with pride. "That's right, baby. Five duckies. You're doing so well."

Tears streamed down her face. Ivy never thought she would see her daughter so joyous and carefree—and learning! She could not remember the last time she had even seen her smile, at least not since she discovered the animal picture book in a car they had used for shelter.

There was so little joy left in this new world.

Sadie was never supposed to happen. For years, Ivy and her husband attempted to conceive a child, only to find out that she was physically unable because of the endometriosis she had developed in her teens. While Kent was devastated, Ivy was secretly content. She never wanted children. Kent wanted a large family much like the one he was raised in, and she was perfectly fine living their life together with a few dogs and a healthier bank account. She entertained the idea before marriage and even went along with the attempts, but ultimately never put her heart into it. She never voiced these feelings to her husband, but she had an inkling after her physician's results, he knew. She was terrified it would drive them apart, and he would not be attracted to her any longer, but ultimately, it did not. Things pretty much stayed the same. Kent focused on his job and improving their home and their life together, and Ivy went back to school to learn to be a hairdresser. But the thoughts were always there. She often wondered how much he thought about it—if he resented her or wished they'd never married.

She thought about a lot of those things while the men in the raiding convoy forcefully took turns on her. For months, along with dozens of other young women, Ivy was repeatedly raped and forced into horrible acts with escaped convicts, bikers, and various other heavily armed lunatics that had brazenly embraced the new world they were gifted. She had no other choice. They fed her and gave her a place to sleep, but she was expected to keep the men—and some of the women—satisfied. When the women refused or attacked any of their suitors, they were shot and left on the roadside. It would not be long before another town would roll by and provide more warm bodies for their urges. It was a nightmare she feared would never escape.

The pregnancy was shocking and utterly devastating. There was absolutely no way she could let a child be born into a world where not only had people turned into primitive cavemen, but they also had to live a life where they would only know captivity. But...there was some part of her that was curious. How it was possible she could conceive at all? She was told it was medically impossible. Yet here she was, expecting a child of some random deviant and not the man she still loved.

Ivy truly hoped Kent had not turned into one of those horrible creatures the caravan mercilessly slaughtered.

She hoped he was still out there. Surviving.

Sadie reached down to scoop up one of the skeletal ducklings.

"Hey, hey, hey!" Ivy stopped her. "Don't touch that."

Her daughter shrugged, unfazed, and continued skipping down the path.

Though none of the primates remained living, Sadie was thrilled by the chimpanzees. They cracked open her book and found the various photos and details of the animals, which Ivy had her slowly read out loud on her own. Sadie shrieked with laughter at her mother's attempts at a bowlegged, arm-curling monkey impersonation.

"What did they sound like, Mommy?"

"Well, they hooted, I guess. Like *hooo hooo hoooooo!*"

Her daughter mimicked Ivy's movements and *hooted* and chirped as though she had seen the creatures many times before. Ivy joined in the fun as the deceased watched on.

They explored many more enclosures, and though most of the smaller wildlife and birds were nowhere to be seen, many of the bigger creatures were exactly where the zookeepers had left them. Because their open-air surroundings were covered in grass and vegetation, the zebras and gazelles appeared as though they had outlasted many of their neighbors. Likely died of dehydration.

The trees surrounding the giraffe exhibit had been picked clean, leaving the gentle giants to huddle together and expire while waiting for their humans to come back.

The reptile house was unfortunately locked up.

The zoo's lone hippopotamus lay unmoving in a black, soupy pool.

Ivy taught Sadie how to roar like a lion, to caw like a parrot, bah like a sheep. At the playground, she showed her daughter how to crawl up the jungle gym and slide down the slide. She watched as her little girl swung higher and higher on the swing set, all by herself. Her little feet touched the sky.

For the first time in her two years on earth, she witnessed her daughter having fun.

In that moment, they were not surviving. They were not searching for food, hotwiring cars, or looking for a safe place to stay from the primitives or her malicious capturers. They were mother and daughter enjoying a day at the zoo.

They were happy.

Fortunately, Ivy's assailants did not much care if she was pregnant or not. They had plenty of girls to take her spot. They let her carry her child to full term, and the doctors they kept on staff helped her birth a healthy baby girl she named Sadie, after Kent's mother. She had kept the name in mind because her husband had been fond of it. It just seemed right, regardless of him not being her father. It kept his memory and her hopes alive.

If she was going to go through with it, she refused to raise her child in this living hell. Sadie would be taken from her and God knew what would be done with her, while her mother went back to being a community whore. She would not allow it. She befriended the doctor—Dr. Kelso Owen—who had helped her in labor and, together with her newborn, slipped away and escaped as the caravan was busy marauding a small town outside of Jackson, Mississippi. Together, they spent the next several months getting as far away from their capturers as possible. They had very little in weapons, and Ivy had to become a good shot very quickly. With the old man's help and guidance, Ivy and Sadie managed to stay healthy and relatively safe. Dr. Owen was not as lucky. He was older and sickly, and he unfortunately caught pneumonia and passed away in their travels. Sadie and her newborn spent the next two years on the road. She fought when she had to. Stole when she needed. Killed any primitive that came near her baby.

Before she knew it, they were back home.

As their day came to a close, Ivy led Sadie back to the entrance of the park. Much to her surprise, her daughter did not cry or pout. She grinned and skipped all the way up to the gift shop.

"Can I...?"

Ivy hesitated but gave in and let her enter the dark store front. She followed her in, but her daughter turned and held up her hand.

"I can do it by myself! I'm a big girl, Mommy."

A sob caught in Ivy's throat. "Yes. Yes, you are." She gently ran her fingers over Sadie's cheek. "Okay. You can go in by yourself. But be careful. I'll be right here waiting for you."

Her daughter smiled and closed the door behind her.

For several minutes, Ivy watched her through the dirt smudged window as she picked through various untouched toys and clothing. Eventually she stepped away and walked back to the lobby area, giving Sadie her space but still keeping an eye on her. She found a bench and sighed as she sat down.

Before she could stop herself, she wept. They were not tears of sadness. She had not felt this relaxed, this carefree and happy, for what seemed like ages. She knew the feeling would not last. Just past those exit doors was a harsh, unavoidable reality. Though she had not seen any sort of life in quite some time, by no means did it cease to exist. But for one special day, they could pretend that every animal was still there. That the monkeys were still swinging on their ropes. That the birds chirped, and the lion stood proud on his rock and roared at onlookers. Turtles basked in sunlight by the lake. A peacock's cry echoing through the park. She was able to show her little miracle that they could pretend and be happy—

Something hard struck her temple. A blinding white light exploded in her eyes. She yelped and fell forward off the bench but managed to not pass out from the pain. She sucked in deep, uneven breaths. Blood trickled down her face, sprinkling the concrete. Vision swimming, she turned to see a nude, female primitive charging out of the bushes, both hands full of rocks.

"*Aaaaughaaaa! Meeeaaannnaaaggghhh!*"

Large stones fell like rain, striking her arms and chest.

Ivy quickly rose to her feet and reached for the curved handle of her machete, plucking the large blade from her side bag. The emaciated primitive closed in, chattering and snapping her blackened gums. Her sour musk permeated the air. Ivy swung the blade and connected with the woman's cheek. The machete cut effortlessly through her face, and blood and teeth flew through the air.

The woman fell to her knees and howled through her newly widened mouth. Ivy moved to swing the blade again, but the primitive was quicker. Arms wrapped tight around her waist, the woman's forehead slammed into her stomach. Ivy gasped for air as her back met the ground. The primitive continued to smash her own skull over and over into Ivy's chest. Her arm's flailed, clawing at any part of Ivy they could find. Grunting, Ivy seized the primitive's throat and lifted her up enough to wedge her knee into the woman's chest. She pushed with all her strength. The primitive howled and vomited dark bile as she rose higher in the air.

Before she could cause any more commotion, Ivy aimed for her neck and swung the machete. The first cut sliced deep, but with a second, two-handed grip she nearly took the woman's head clean off. Blood sprayed over the concrete and all over Ivy's face and jacket. The primitive's body stiffened, her head hanging on by a thin strip of skin, then collapsed on its side.

Ivy pushed her body off and leapt to her feet. She stood her ground, waiting for more primitives to show themselves.

The door to the gift shop swung open, and Sadie sauntered out with a smile and arm full of merchandise. Ivy wiped her machete off on the grass, then placed it back in her bag next to the picture book. Her daughter stopped and stiffened, eyes growing wide.

"Mommy...?"

"Everything's okay, sweetheart. I'm okay. Mommy just had to protect us."

"Bad people?"

"Yes, but Mommy took care of it."

Relaxing, her daughter understood and nodded. She had seen her mother fight off primitives many times before. At this point for the two-year-old, it was almost old hat.

"I got this for you." She handed her mother a red pullover hoodie with the zoo's name and logo on the chest.

Ivy grinned and switched her blood-covered jacket with fresh new clothing. Sadie also changed, switching to a smaller hoodie that matched her mother's. She hugged and played with her new stuffed black bear while Ivy brushed and braided her hair.

As they walked back through the exit into the parking lot, she asked, "Can we go to another, Mommy? Please?"

Ivy did not even have to think about her answer. "Of course, honey. Of course."

If she was not mistaken, the next zoo was well over a hundred miles and a whole other state away. But for Sadie, her little miracle, she would walk another two hundred. Whatever it took.

Anything to keep her smiling.

Story Notes:

The death of author J.F. Gonzalez hit me pretty hard. I'll admit I didn't know Jesus personally, only having met him twice, but I've always credited him, along with Brian Keene and Tim Lebbon, as the reason I write at all. His work was hugely influential in my coming up as writer. His works like *The Beloved*, *Survivor*, and *The Corporation* left an indelible mark on me as did his collections *Old Ghosts and Other Revenants* and *When the Darkness Falls*. He was a fantastic author who maybe didn't have the readership he deserved while alive, though, fortunately for us, Brian Keene is in charge of his literary estate and is painstakingly reprinting his wonderful back catalog for a new generation of readers. Which brings us to this story.

    Several years ago, Brian had announced he was putting together a charity anthology for Mr. Gonzalez's estate, and he wanted contributions for this book from fellow authors who either knew Jesus personally or revered his work. The anthology was to be called *Clickers Forever* and would highlight his popular, giant crab monster series *Clickers*, along with pieces of non-fiction about the man himself from his close friends. I badly wanted to write a story for this, but, admittedly, I wasn't the biggest fan of those books and I struggled with forming an idea for a story, so I abandoned the idea of sending something Keene's way. Fast forward a few months, and I was visiting my girlfriend (now wife) and friends in Pennsylvania for my birthday, and Keene joined us for dinner at a local Mexican restaurant. He asked me why I hadn't submitted anything for the anthology. I shrugged, embarrassed, and told him I didn't think I was good enough to have anything accepted. He thought about it and said he didn't receive any stories from anyone set in the world of Gonzalez's novel *Primitive*. "Can you write me a story from that book?" Of course I agreed, and then I sat there the rest of the meal fighting the urge to vomit. What the hell was I going to do? I hadn't read that novel since it came out years before. I rushed home and re-read the book, and fortunately fell in love with the novel all over again. But I still didn't have an idea whatsoever. One night I was looking through a file on my computer and found an abandoned story that I had only written maybe fifty words in, and something in that snippet immediately sparked the idea of the story you just read.

My wife and I love to visit zoos and have been to more than we can count. I distinctly remember walking through one one day, seeing the children joyously celebrating the animals, and thinking what if a child was running through a zoo of dead animals and was equally as excited? Add into that the post-apocalyptic world of Primitive and everything seemed to fit perfectly. I mentally based the fictional zoo on Mesker Park Zoo, which is the zoo from my hometown in Evansville, Indiana. I'm really proud of this story.

CATALOG

Andrea Ricci leaned in to open his mailbox—then immediately recoiled.

Even though the mid-summer sun blazed high above his bald head, bright enough for those last few remaining hairs to shine, the inside of the compartment was as black as a windowless closet. Sweat dripping down his face, he stared hard into the box, unsure if he should reach inside and take what was his. He did not have to know what it was. He just knew it was *his*.

"Andy, hon? Are you going to help me bring in groceries, or are you going to stare at the mail all day?"

His wife's words barely registered, distant and choppy, as if spoken over an ocean. Ready to see, he reached in and felt his mail. He carefully pulled it out into the light.

"Andy? Hello?"

The catalog's cover was glossy and black, and even though he treated it like a snake ready to strike, it felt good in his calloused, arthritic hands. Obedient. His eyes clicked across the three block words printed across the cover.

"*Ciao?* Earth to Andrea?"

A drop of sweat fell from his nose onto the cover. It *sizzled*.

"Goddamn it, Andy! Are you going to help me or not?"

Andrea blinked, and his wife's voice was suddenly back in the front yard with him. He glanced sideways, not moving his head. "*Sì, sì, sì*, I hear you. Just…one moment…*per favore*.

Standing by the open car door of their '74 Firebird, Donna huffed and shook her head. She adjusted her weight so it wasn't all on her heavily casted leg and then linked her arm through several plastic grocery bags. She mumbled loudly, "Sure, sure, sure, just one minute. Absolutely. You'd think, 'Hey, maybe I should help my wife who's got a broken leg, but no, I have to admire the water bill just a *little* longer.' Nope, nothing to see here, folks."

"What's there nothing to see of?"

Andrea cringed at the new voice, not having to turn around to see its owner. But he did anyway.

"Kirk!" Donna beamed. "Oh, nothing. Just taking in groceries. Normal Saturday. How are you doing, Father? Keeping cool, I hope?"

"Oh, as well as can be in ninety-five-degree weather, I suppose. One thing, dear Donna: please don't take the Lord's name in vain. He may have his AC going up there, but He can still hear you."

She smiled and quickly crossed herself.

The priest nodded and then turned to Andrea with tight lips. "*Ciao*, Andrea. How's retirement these days, *mio amico*?"

Stifling a growl, Andrea glared at the plain-clothed pastor with red-rimmed eyes. He took deep, controlled breaths, wishing the man away, far away, then turned back to the glossy black item in his hands.

He heard them both shrug. Pastor Kirk then asked, "Listen, Donna, is it okay if I place one of these in your yard? As you can see, I've got one in every yard in the neighborhood. It's mostly for Fourth of July, you know, getting in the spirit and whatnot, but also for…Luca."

"Absolutely," she said. "That's a wonderful gesture."

"Fantastic, thank you. Andrea, is it okay with you?"

Without looking at him, Andrea gave him a slight wave. His heart pounded, his mouth cotton dry. He heard the man walk down their gravel driveway to the sidewalk, heard his grunts as he bent over in their front yard. Eyes burning, he rolled the catalog in his grip and stormed off to the side kitchen door. Before stepping inside, he stole a quick glance toward the Father in his front yard.

The man pressed a foot-long wooden stick into the grass. The tiny American flag stapled to the top whipped in the breeze.

Kirk looked up to him and nodded solemnly.

Andrea closed the door behind him.

***

After speaking with Kirk for a few more minutes outside, Donna hobbled into the house with several overfilled bags of groceries painfully linked across both arms. She angrily dropped the food onto the tiled kitchen floor. His back turned toward her, her husband stood at the sink with the mail he had taken from the front box. He didn't react, didn't acknowledge her presence. That pissed her off more.

"What the hell was *that* all about?"

Silence.

"Andrea, *idiota*! Drop the mail and talk to me!"

His shoulders hitched like he was hyperventilating, his breathing heavy and laborious. She went to grab the single black magazine he gripped in his hands, but he spun his shoulder and growled. *Growled.*

"You've got some nerve!" she cried. "What is your malfunction, Andy? You're being rude as all hell today. First you stiff me on helping bring the groceries in, then your boorish attitude toward Kirk. Now you growl at me like some wild animal? You mind explaining yourself?"

His heavy breathing halted, he rolled the magazine up and gripped it with both hands. He turned to face her, both sweat and regret dripping down his face. "I'm…sorry, *amore mio.*"

"*Sorry?* You're *sorry*? For which one?"

He sighed. "All of them."

She stood there, incredulous, waiting for more. When she didn't receive it, she went on. "What has gotten into you lately, Andy? You're so distant and angry. I feel like I can't even talk to you anymore. Is it…?" She sighed. "Is it Luca?"

She could almost see the glass behind his eyes shatter. It was rounding up to the sixth anniversary of their son's death, their baby boy, their twenty-three-year-old, Afghanistan-bound soldier, and the years still hadn't been kind. He was their only child, the light of Andrea's life, the proud smile across his face…and it was all gone in a fiery instant.

Andrea nodded, refusing to show any emotion. He was old school like that.

Anger pushed aside, she went to hug her husband, but he shook his head and waved her away. She stood back and watched him struggle. It was a struggle for her too. The last several years had been a crash course through hell, considerable pain she wouldn't dare wish on anyone. With the loss of their son in the war, and Andrea unwillingly selling his company, he just wasn't the same man she married all those years ago.

It was 1977 the first time she laid eyes on Andrea Ricci, and just like his surname, he wore a long frock of wild red hair, which was quite rare for Italians back then. He was fresh off the boat, the first of his family to come to the states in search of his 'American Dream.' His dream was to work on cars, and though he didn't have access to the Lamborghinis and Ferraris of his homeland, he was perfectly content in learning the inner workings of "lesser American-made tin cans." After a few years of traveling the states, he had found himself in Indianapolis, where he had wandered into her father's auto body shop. And for her, it was love at first sight. He barely spoke English, but after proving he could work just as hard as the other men in the shop, he was quickly hired on. At the time, she was working there as the receptionist, storing her paychecks toward college tuition, but after Andrea was brought on, she spent *a lot* less time at her desk.

It wasn't long before he had learned the language, and it was even quicker he had taken her heart. The romance was hasty and strong, and she relished those nights she would hear sweet foreign nothings whispered in her ears. Her father didn't approve, but she didn't care. They were in love, and if it meant dropping out of school and moving somewhere new for Andrea to start his own shop, then so be it. By '82, they were married and had settled south in Poseyville, Indiana, where he could be the only auto body shop in town. The small town quickly gained trust in the crafty outsider and everyone knew his name. Ricci's Auto and Glass became everything to Andrea, and Andrea was everything to Donna. That is until Luca.

They had decided to wait several years until they had a child. Andrea had been a workaholic, and his long hours at the shop wouldn't have been prudent for their future. By the time Luca Ottone Ricci was born, Donna wasn't sure how Andrea would receive him. But the boy became his moon and his stars, and Donna would lay awake every night, listening to Andrea's dreams of passing down his passions, of working side-by-side with his *figlio*. He was a different man with Luca in his arms… and now a much different man without him.

With their son killed in the line of duty, Andrea was a broken man. Their personal life was in shambles, and his work began to suffer for it. His ever-reliant clients started going elsewhere. And when the slick businessman with deep pockets came in from Louisville with an offer they just couldn't refuse, he was forced into an early retirement. He didn't want to sell the business; it was everything to him. But she talked him into it, hoping the money and his newly freed-up time would help them mend their wounds and help them become scars.

It only made it worse.

Here he was, a shell of his former self. His beautiful, long, ruddy red hair gone, replaced by a russet horseshoe and a slick shine. He didn't sleep much, spent more time tinkering in the garage. Spoke only in snippets.

His American Dream was gone. "*Morto e sepolto.*"

And it made her deepest, darkest secret all that much harder to hold.

"Listen," she said, reaching out to touch his shoulder, "I know you're hurting. I'm hurting too. I miss him so much." Tears dripped down her cheeks.

His chest shook as he fought his own tears. He gave her a slight nod, not meeting her eyes. "It...hurts."

She pressed her face into his wide shoulder. "I know it does. It hasn't gotten any easier, has it? I keep thinking time will ease the pain, but it's still there. It's still...*bubbling.*"

He rolled the magazine tighter in his hands.

She looked up to him. "We just have to keep working at it. We'll get through this, *amore mio.*"

For the first time in a while, he gave her a smile, though a sad one. "*Amore mio.*"

Donna wiped her eyes and hobbled back over to the groceries on the floor. "By the way, Father Kirk invited us to his cookout on July third."

Andrea's smile immediately faded. He sneered and waved her away.

"Come on, Andy. Everyone in the neighborhood will be there. People have been asking about you, you know? They miss you. You need to get out of the house more. It'll be good for you."

He sighed, obviously done fighting for the day. "Fine."

"Good. Now, you either help me put this food away, or I'm going to fall down the stairs again and break my other leg, and you can put them all up yourself.

***

Unfortunately, nothing had changed. Over the course of the next week, her husband, the man she adored to the moon and back, remained as distant as ever. She tried anything to brighten his mood. She cooked his favorite meals of Ribollita and Beef Braciole, both of which remained cold and picked at. She invited friends over for drinks and conversation, but the best she got from Andrea was distant stares. Even lovemaking, something they both could have won trophies for in their twenties, was mechanical at best. Sure, they were much older now, with a lot more aches and pains, but it never stopped Andrea from giving her all he had, even outside of the bedroom. Nothing satisfied him. Nothing brought joy or pleasure or even a hint of his old self to the surface.

The only constant was that damn catalog.

Many times when she couldn't find him around the house, she would discover him in the garage, thumbing through its pages at his cluttered work bench. The few times she asked to see it, she was met with growls, always quickly hiding it behind his back. At first, she thought maybe it was a dirty magazine. She wasn't fully on board with the idea, but maybe it would help his spirits in some abstract way. She knew that wasn't the case. The few times she got a look at it, its cover was black and glossy with only a few white lettered words across the top. Never did she get to see the contents inside.

But it wasn't just in the garage. There were other times she found him sitting in his beloved Firebird in the driveway. Once out behind the yard barn. The night before last standing by himself in the school yard up the street from their house.

Nearly forty years of marriage, and her husband felt like a complete stranger again.

***

"I knew it!"

Donna muted the TV when Andrea, red faced and sweaty, stormed tornado-like into the house. He slammed the front door behind him.

"You knew what?" she asked. "What's wrong?"

Fuming, he stomped back and forth on the other side of the coffee table, hands on his hips, his head bobbing as if it were on a spring. "I knew it! *Maledizione*, I knew it!"

She stood up and reached out to touch him, but he shouldered away her hand. "Will you please calm down and tell me what's wrong? You're going to give your damn fool self a heart attack!"

"*Che palle!*" he yelled. "It happened again, Donna. They slashed my tire again. Again!"

"Who? Slashed your tires?"

He continued to pace. "Who do you think? Horning! Th-that *figlio di puttana*! He did it again!"

She sighed. "For Christ's sake, Andy. Horning did *not* slash your tires."

"But he did! And it was he and his goons that did it the last time—in the exact same spot, no less!"

This wasn't the first time Andrea had made such wild claims about Nathan Horning, the man who purchased Andy's shop and life's work. Andrea never wanted to step away from the business he spent decades building, the clientele he worked so hard to retain, and the very thing he wanted to pass down to their son. But Luca's death, cheaper pricing, and his stubbornness to hire apprentices took people's loyalty elsewhere. When the money was too good to pass up, Donna begged him to sign on the dotted line. Maybe it was the wrong thing to do. Maybe the effects of it were now tearing her husband apart, but it only made sense at the time. It kept Andrea home with her, where they got to spend more time together, something they hadn't done since Reagan was in office. It was time for them to mourn Luca together, instead of him working his feelings away under a car hood.

"Andy, I love you, you know I do, but you can't keep doing this."

He stared at her incredulously. "Do what? Speak the truth? That Horning is a damn fool if he thinks he can continue to get away with this!"

She shook her head.

"It's not just me, Donna! Others are saying it too! Just yesterday, Mitchel across the street says his car door won't unlock anymore, and now he must take it to the shop to get fixed. Joni next door say her windshield is cracked, and she have no idea how it happened."

"All accidents, Andy. All explainable."

"All *explainable*? What about the hole in my tire?"

She shrugged. "Probably a nail! Come on. You better than anybody should know how this works. How many nails have you pulled from tires over the last forty years?"

"It was no nail!" he screamed. "Nails don't put inch long holes in the side of the damn tire!"

She threw her hands up, frustrated and fed up. "Then I don't know, Andy. I don't have a good answer for you. But I do know that Horning isn't going around breaking people's cars just for the fun of it."

Andrea surprised her when he lashed out and kicked the reclining chair behind him. He yelped and hopped on one foot. "*Merda!*"

"For Christ's sake, will you settle down before you break your damn foot? You're acting like a crazy man."

He eyed her through his pain. "*Ma vaffanculo!*"

Donna paused and glared at her husband; hands locked onto her hips. Not once in their nearly four decades of marriage had he ever told her to "go fuck herself," in any language. She said nothing when he went silent. They stared at one another, and even through his rage, she knew he regretted his words. He sighed and opened his mouth, then closed it and walked down to the basement.

***

Donna awoke from a dead sleep. She hadn't quite hit the age where she needed to get up throughout the night to use the bathroom—not like Andrea—but something else roused her, something off. Her eyes snapped open.

The first thing she noticed was the lack of body heat coming from the other side of the bed. Andrea typically slept right against her back, most nights with his arm around her midsection.

The other thing was the breathing.

She quietly rolled over and found Andrea sitting upright on the edge of the bed. He was facing away from her, his silhouette haloing in the moonlit window. Hunched over, his shoulders moved up and down with his slow, laborious breaths. His arms trembled.

"Andy, hon? What are you doing? What time is it?"

He immediately stopped. He sluggishly lifted his head and ever so slightly turned toward her. The light obscured his eyes. "Nothing, *caro*. Go back to sleep." He leaned over and opened the top drawer of his nightstand and placed the black glossy catalog inside before closing it. Gingerly, he laid back down and covered himself. Within moments he was fast asleep and snoring.

Donna, on the other hand, stayed awake for a very long time.

***

The sun was hot, the grill was smoking, and Andrea's guts were on fire.

He hated this, every Goddamn second of it, but he didn't have much of a choice. Donna was desperate to get him out of the house and into the bright, harsh world outside. Several days after the fact, and it still ate him up that he had chosen such cruel words to throw at her in his rage. He loved her more than life itself, and if going to Father Kirk's barbeque for the day would make her happy, then a smile he would wear.

But the smile was short lived. Three hours in, and the overcooked burgers sat like fat lumps of charcoal in his stomach. He hadn't wanted to eat—honestly, he hadn't much of an appetite for some time—but Donna's concern for his health forced him to choke down the blackened, unseasoned meat. He didn't want to be there. Every voice, every burst of laughter or clicking of tongue was like a bullet to the brain.

He stood at the corner of the porch, watching everyone below. He knew every face, every bad joke and haircut. They all went to the same Catholic Church at the end of the block, the one the man behind the grill looked after. Like him, Kirk was in his mid-sixties and was as bald as the day was long. They met early on when Donna and he moved south and set up shop. They needed a place of worship, and Father Kirk, who lived three houses down from their new home, had welcomed them with open arms. They were close at first. They fished together, drank together, and when Luca was born, he stood bedside with them, blessing their son as he joined the world. And somewhere along the way, they drifted apart.

Religion had begun to slip away from Andrea the older he got, spending more time away from the church after Luca died. He couldn't stand the sight of it, the terrible memories it brought forth every time he prayed. God couldn't keep his only son safe on the other side of the world, and all the prayers in the world didn't change the fact he came home in an American flag-wrapped wooden box. Oddly, Father Kirk seemed to have been hit just as hard by losing Luca. The man wailed with them at the funeral, unable to be the pillar of strength a man of God should be in his flock's time of need. The Father held Donna close as Luca was placed six feet underground. No matter his own pain, it was Andrea's job to be the protector and the shoulder to cry on...and Father Kirk had taken that from him. He never let Donna know of his feelings. It was something best kept tightly sealed.

From behind the grill, Kirk looked up at the deck balcony to Andrea. The man gave him a nod and a tight-lipped smile.

Sweat dripping down his face, Andrea looked away.

Donna climbed the deck steps, grunting as she struggled with her cast, and joined his side. She handed him a freshly opened Peroni, which he waved away.

"Why don't you come down and join us, hon?" she asked. "The McGilligans have been asking about you. Mason said he wants a cornhole rematch from last year. Says you cheated and wants a fair fight this time. Said something about 'keeping those big-ass feet of yours behind the line'."

Andrea shook his head.

Donna sighed and put her arm around his waist. "Why not, Andy? You've been up here all day, glaring at everyone like some angry King. Please come down and be sociable. It would mean the world to me."

His heart began to thump like dancing stallions. His hands gripped the air. Breath was short. He glanced down at Father Kirk, and the man's eyes continued to linger on them both.

"Okay," he squeezed out. "I'll be down in moment. My stomach is bothering me. *Davvero male.*"

She nodded. "Okay. Bathroom's inside, just past the kitchen, on the left."

Andrea shakenly leaned over and kissed his wife's forehead. "I love you, *caro. Molto molto.*"

"*Molto molto,*" she said with a grin.

"*Un momento.*" He turned and hurried inside.

Andrea closed the sliding glass doors and relished the chilled interior of the house, the thick hair on his arms standing straight up. He stepped into the kitchen, opened the freezer door, and stuck his head in, letting the frosty air cool his sweat beads. When his breathing was back to normal, he closed the door and stepped out into the living room toward the bathroom.

The living room was small, with couches so old there were weathered holes in the seat cushions. An eighties style box television sat on the floor, the corner of its screen cracked into spiderwebs. Save for a few dusty landscape paintings, the walls were bare and dusty. He realized he had known Kirk for so many years and had never thought to ask about his family. The man had never married, had never spoken of parents or living relatives. The lack of life across the walls and tabletops painted a sad, disheartening existence. When they still spoke regularly,

Kirk had always come to their house. Other than the occasional cookouts; this may have been his first time inside the Catholic priest's home. Andrea guessed he didn't blame Kirk for not wanting others over. There was nothing to show off.

That was until Andrea took the door on the right instead of the left.

He clicked open the door, expecting the bathroom, and was instead greeted by the musty smell of a bedroom. The curtains were drawn, but the midday sun still bled across the room in hazy lines. The bed was unkempt and filthy, the uncovered pillows stained yellow with sweat and drool. The man's clothes were everywhere, his frocks piled haphazardly on a folding chair in the far corner. But none of this held his attention.

Andrea's eyes were glued to walls. Dozens upon dozens of framed pictures were hung about the coffee-colored room, all in various sizes and shapes.

All containing Luca.

Andrea's breath caught in this throat. Every picture contained the various faces of the son he lost. The faces of the newborn he helped deliver in the hospital, swaddled and held in the arms of Kirk. The cheerful expressions of the toddler playing in the snow, being pushed down the hill behind this very house. The eyes peering out behind locks of long red hair from an angry teenager, taken just behind Andrea and Donna's heads at the boy's high school graduation. Pictures of Andrea and Luca....of Luca and Donna...of Luca and Kirk. Various Polaroid's were taped to the walls, showing far away deserts and soldiers in full combat gear. Pictures Andrea had never received in those few, long years of Luca's service. There were other photos too. Ones with happy smiles of two people that were never married, two people never meant to touch.

He began to sweat again. The room spun. Hands gripped the doorframe.

Andrea carefully closed the bedroom door, then walked home, stepping over each planted American flag along the way.

***

Donna stayed at the party for a few more hours after she knew Andrea had abruptly left. At first, she was furious, having to lie to her friends that Andy was probably tired or sick, but the company of friends eventually dulled her anger. Catherine

Lowelstein helped her walk home, but she made the trek down the stairs to the basement all by herself.

She found Andrea slumped behind the lacquered oak bar in the far corner. In front of him, an ice filled glass of amber liquid. Behind him and spread across the bar top, several half-empty bottles of various shapes and colors. Other than the dim spotlights above him, the basement was shrouded in black, the only light from the small rectangular window by the liquor cabinet.

Donna pulled a barstool out and sat down. She stared at him, but he refused to meet her eyes. "Care to explain yourself?"

He lifted his glass and took a slow, drawn-out sip before replacing it on the bar top.

"At first I was worried sick about you," she said. "You looked terrible on the deck, and I figured you went to use the bathroom or sit in the air conditioning or something, but I went in, and you were nowhere to be found. It was embarrassing, Andy, having to tell all of our neighbors you up and left and I—"

"Is Luca my son?"

The words stopped her cold in her tracks. A thousand tiny fingers skittered up her spine. Her flesh went cold.

"Excuse me?"

He took another sip, then drained his glass. "You heard me," he slurred.

"No, I don't think I did."

He sighed, pouring himself another glass, this time with clear liquid. "*Is* he or *isn't* he my son?"

Her tongue felt too big for her mouth. "Well, of course he is. Why would you ask such a thing, Andy?"

Another drink and he finally met her eyes. They were so distant they seemed to look right through her. "You would not lie to me, *sì*? You would not tell me untruths?"

"No." She shook her head, maybe a little too hard. "Of course not."

"You know...I came to this country with nothing. *Niente.* No money, no home. I come to look for the one thing I hear about all my life in Milan. The American Dream. You, *mio caro*, you were born with it. It is given to you. Me? I had to earn it. I worked hard for it. I learn your language, your customs, your shitty automobiles. I earned everything I have."

She reached out to touch his hand, but he gently pulled it away.

"I only wanted the simple things," he continued. "I wanted money. I wanted home and business. I wanted wife and child—a son to give my passion to. And it's all gone. Luca? Dead. My car shop? Gone. My wife—"

"Is here with you right now and is not going anywhere."

He frowned and cocked his head. "Are you sure about that?"

"Yes!" she yelled. "Andy...listen... I know this has been a very difficult few years for you—for the *both* of us—and I know it seems like the world is crumbling around you, but I am here for you. I always have been. We're going to get through this. I promise."

His eyes threatened tears, but they never came. He stuttered a short breath and looked away. "I'm sorry I was not always there for you."

"Andy, it's—"

"I'm sorry I wasn't in Luca's life more. I'm sorry I worked so much and spent so little time at home. I was a bad father and husband."

Donna scooped up his hand with both of hers. "Andy, stop. The past is the past. Despite what you think, I wouldn't change it for anything. We've had a great life together, we built a business together from nothing, made a beautiful baby boy together—"

Andrea tore his hand from her loving grip, instead going for his liquor. He drained the glass in two gulps and slammed it hard on the wooden bar top. Donna yelped, nearly falling from her stool. A few moments of silence passed before he whispered, "It's getting late. You should get some sleep."

She stared at him as he gazed out the window. Her breath was short, and her stomach continued to somersault. She went to stand, and her eyes caught something. At the far corner of the bar, the catalog sat rolled up like a Sunday newspaper. She stared at it for a few moments before reaching out to grab it.

Andrea's hand shot out and snatched it first. He slowly pulled it toward himself, then placed it underneath the bar.

Short of breath, she hobbled over to the steps. She turned back to her husband. "I love you, Andy. Very much."

Without looking at her, he whispered back, "*Molto molto,*" then took another drink.

***

Early the next morning, the day of July fourth, there was a knock at the front door. Donna was sitting at the dining room table by herself, putting together a five-hundred-piece jigsaw puzzle of an old Thomas Kinkade painting she had once bought at the mall. They weren't expecting anyone, at least not until later when her sister and nieces would pick her up to watch the fireworks down at the riverfront.

"Andy, hon, can you get that please?" When she didn't receive an answer, she repeated, "Andy, please answer the door. My leg is bothering me, and I don't want to get up." Still nothing.

She shakily stood with a groan, then grabbed her crutches and gingerly hobbled to the living room. She hadn't needed crutches in a few weeks, but the pain in her broken ankle was at a high that morning, and no amount of pain medication was dulling it.

Another knock, this time more insistent.

"All right, all right, I'm on my way," she yelled. "Crippled woman coming through."

There was one more heavy knock before Donna could reach the door. She unlocked the handle and pulled it open. Beyond the screen door, nobody was there.

Only a box.

She opened the outer door and frowned. Not a single soul in sight, no one on foot or even a delivery truck speeding away. She stared at the hefty sized cardboard box. Maybe three feet long, two feet high. Other than the initials **ASC** in large, black letters on the lid, there was no writing on the box. With a foot nudge she confirmed it was much heavier than it looked. She adjusted her crutches and began to bend over to pick it up—

—when Andrea pushed her aside and took it himself. She stepped back and let him bring the box inside.

"What is that? I didn't think the post office delivered on holidays?"

Without answering, he continued to carry his package through the living room into the dining room, where he nudged open the basement steps.

"Andy?" she asked quietly. "Are you going to speak to me today?"

He stopped on the first step down, his face remaining forward.

"Andy...please talk to me. I can't handle this silent treatment. It's not fair."

Andrea remained quiet, his shoulders slowly moving up and down with his breaths.

"Fine," she croaked, stifling the hitch in her chest. "Go hide away then. Be by yourself. I'll just go out tonight with Monica and the girls by myself, and we'll enjoy the fireworks without you."

He still said nothing. Then he dropped his head and continued down the stairs.

***

The dull pain in Donna's leg had become a beastly roar by the time she was dropped off at home. The girls, eleven and thirteen, were both so excited to see the fireworks. It had become a tradition over the last decade or so that her sister would bring the girls down from Indianapolis to see the fireworks on the Ohio River, but Mother Nature had other plans. From the time they left the house, the rain came down hard for several hours. When it appeared it wasn't stopping, she was brought back home to rest. The pain had become unbearable, and since the fireworks were now being pushed back until later that night, there was no reason to stay up.

The house was dark and seemingly empty when she entered through the side kitchen door. She sat her purse down on the table, along with the red, white, and blue top hat little Kate had given her to wear, and made a beeline for the medicine cabinet in the bathroom.

Someone stepped out in front of her.

Donna yelped and stumbled backwards into the wall.

Andrea slid out from the bathroom doorway and stared at her. In one hand, a plastic cup of water, in the other, two white pills.

"Jesus Christ Almighty, Andy! You nearly put me in an early grave."

"Sorry," he mumbled.

She stared at the contents in his hands. "For me?"

He nodded and carefully handed them to her.

She thanked him and quickly downed the pills one after the other, then emptied the glass.

"*Nessun problema.*" He took the cup back and tossed it in the waste can.

When her heart rate dribbled back down, she asked, "Can we please talk?"

He shook his head no, his mouth a tight, horizontal line. Placing his hand on her lower back, he guided her toward the bedroom. "Not tonight, *caro*. We sleep on it."

Donna nodded, not wanting to push the matter. It felt good to be touched by him again, even a little bit, and maybe, just maybe, they could begin to work it out tomorrow.

She smiled.

***

It was like climbing out of a pit of mud. Her hands reached for the edge, trying to pull herself over, but she continued to slip further down. She repeated the process, over and over, until she finally got her leg over the top and began to pull herself out. Her eyes opened, albeit slowly, and the world around her surged like heat waves. No matter how much she blinked, the pillows around her eyes remained soft and impeding. She laid there for a long while, sucking on air with cotton-dry gums. After what seemed like an eternity, she slowly rolled her head to the side.

In the dark of the bedroom, Andrea stood in the far corner by the closet. His back was turned, his forehead leaning in the V of the meeting walls. His shoulders hitched up and down, his breathing erratic.

Donna tried to speak, but only a dry squeak released from her throat.

His head slowly turned toward her, and before she could see his eyes, she tumbled back down into the mud.

***

"All right, gentlemen, listen close. Here are your assignments. Juney, you're on Nottingham tonight. Simon, you go down to… Franklin. Plenty of vehicles down there at the bars. Miles, you take Oaklawn."

"What about me boss?"

"What about you, Brogan?"

"Well, don't I get a street?"

Nathan Horning grinned. "No, you don't."

The kid frowned. "Why the hell not?"

"Because you have a stupid fucking millennial-ass name like *Brogan*, that's why. If you weren't my nephew, I'd have beaten the shit out of you and your Mother for that name."

The other three men cackled in the chairs. Brogan slumped, his face flushing red.

Simon asked, "How long we gotta be out tonight, boss? I mean, it's a holiday, right?"

"Yeah," Juney added. "I've a twelve pack and a big pair of titties calling my name at home."

Nathan frowned, his mood immediately souring. "You guys are done when I fucking say you're done and not a minute sooner. You got it? I already overpay you fucking slugs, the least you can do is go out and do your Goddamn jobs!" He took a breath. "Tell you what, keep track of what you did and where you did it, and whoever has the most vehicles come in by week's end can have the weekend off. Sound good, fucksticks?"

Four smiles blossomed in front of him. "Good. Now get out there and make us some money. And, oh yeah, Brogan. Go with Miles. Maybe you can bring back a better name."

They all stood and left him alone in his office. Finally, he could get back to the important stuff. He lit a cigarette and pulled the fat manila envelope from his side drawer. He tipped it over, and multiple rolls of greenbacks toppled over his desktop. He lifted a handful of twenties and inhaled them.

Business was good.

It had been for quite some time. He ran the perfect outfit. Everyone had cars, right? And cars break down and need new parts, right? So where do you go when the only other place to have such needs met is over thirty miles away? That old wop he bought this shithole from had no idea what a genuine goldmine he sat on. Or maybe he did, but it took a real genius to see it to its full potential. Sure, he hated living in the middle of pig shit Midwest, but money talks, and boy howdy, it was singing a wonderful song lately. A chipped window here, a broken wiper there, and the only service and a smile in town was Horning's Auto Plus.

Outside in the shop, he heard a sharp yelp. Other than the lights in his office, the shop was dark and closed for the night, his mechanics gone for the evening. "Yo, are you guys still out there? Why haven't you left yet?"

Another quick yelp and it went quiet again.

Frowning, Nathan began to stand and reach for the revolver under his desk when a figure appeared from the shade of the hallway. Caught off guard, Nathan froze and gripped the weapon, but when he saw who it was he flopped back in his chair and barked out a laugh. "What are *you* doing here, old man?"

The old Italian man—Andrew...something-or-other—stood before him. Nathan hadn't seen him in quite some time, at least not since fleecing him out of his business a few years back, but he knew for a fact he'd sent his crew out to fuck with his car. He must have been driving out of his way to avoid coming back here. The man somehow looked older, more haggard, with bags under his eyes so large they could fit his dirty laundry.

"We're closed, man. I'm sure you know that. The times haven't changed." Nathan stared at him, and the old man stared back. Other than his heavy breathing, he hadn't spoken a single word.

"What do you want, old man? Can't you see I'm fucking busy? And how did you get in here anyways?" He placed a hand across his money. "Bet you never raked this kind of dough in when you were here, huh?" He snickered.

The old man continued to stare, and that was when Nathan noticed a small splash of red across the man's white shirt near his breast. His eyes dropped down to the long, wooden object in his hand.

Nathan's laughter died. "What the fuck do you plan on doing with that?"

The old man showed him.

***

Kirk startled himself awake from a fitful sleep. Despite the AC going at full blast, his sweating body stuck to the old, unwashed bed sheets. Sleep had eluded him for days now, maybe weeks, but the closer it got to July fourth, the harder it was to exist. For several minutes, he laid there and cried, his tears cooling against his cheeks. And he prayed—by the Father, the Son, and the Holy Spirit, he prayed. Yet God would not answer. He would not bring his son back. Kirk begged to join him.

The bedroom floor creaked.

Kirk's eyes shot wide open and without lifting his head, he looked down toward the doorway.

"A…Andrea?"

A figure stood there, watching over him in the pressing darkness. Kirk didn't have to see his face. He just knew it was him.

He began to cry once more. "I miss him so much, Andy. It's chewing me up inside."

Andrea didn't answer him. He only took a step closer to the bed.

Kirk wept, "I should have told you so long ago. I never should have kept this from you. Andrea…I loved him so much. I loved them both."

Another step.

"I still do."

Andrea gradually crawled onto the bed and sat on Kirk's chest.

"Please…Please, God, let me join him."

His God finally listened.

***

When Donna finally came to and felt strong enough to sit up, she forced her shaking body out of bed. She grabbed for her crutches and, still woozy, managed to get to the bathroom in time to vomit. As the room spun like a top, she wondered just what the hell Andrea had given her before she laid down. It most certainly wasn't her pain medication. Whatever the hell it was put her out for hours, and even though the clock read just after ten, it felt like she had been asleep for days.

She flushed the toilet and carefully hobbled out of the bathroom. The house was pitch black, and when she went for the light switch, nothing happened. She tried the other one in the kitchen, and that too failed her. Unable to find a flashlight, she grabbed a candle from the stand in the hallway and lit it.

"Andy? Where are you?"

She crept through the house by candlelight. At some point, the rain had stopped, and the sound of neighborhood fireworks were going off in the streets—reds, blues, and greens exploding across the sky. Inside, however, was unnervingly quiet.

When Andrea didn't show up, she decided to call her sister to come get her. That was before she noticed the open basement door. Any other time, she wouldn't have had any issue going down the steps, even with her crutches, but the throbbing pain in her leg remained a constant, and every time her walking boot touched the floor, lightning shot up her leg.

"Andy?" she asked the darkness below.

Carefully, she descended the stairs, one tentative step at a time, keeping one hand on the banister, while the other held the candle and cradled her crutches. By the time she reached the bottom, she was dizzy and out of breath. She replaced the crutches under her arms and held out the candle.

Much like the upstairs, the basement was void of life. In the corner, their flat-screen TV and the overstuffed recliners that faced it. Several shelves full of John Wayne DVDs. Picture frames were plastered across the walls, many with the smiling face of her deceased son. A sob hitched in her throat.

Holding back her tears, she spun around to look for the circuit breaker and found herself facing the bar.

And there on the bar was the catalog.

Suspiciously, she hobbled over to the wood topped bar to get a better look. But something about it kept her at a distance. It was as if she were approaching a wild snake, and getting too close might startle it. From a few feet away, the candle's flame leapt across its black glossy cover, and she noticed it was no longer rolled up. It appeared brand new, fresh off the printer. She swallowed and stepped closer to read the three white block lettered words across the top.

AMERICAN SUPPLY CO.

Other than those words, the cover was bare and lifeless. With a trembling hand, she reached out and touched it. When it didn't bite back, she flipped the catalog over, finding a similar motif. Nothing. Not a bar code or their address. Confused, she flipped it back over and began to thumb through its pages.

Every single one was blank.

She let the cover fall back in place and stepped away. This didn't make sense. Why was this empty book the very thing that seemed to rob every bit of Andrea's time and focus? What was he looking at inside those blank pages? What about it kept him up at night?

She spotted an open box on the floor behind the bar, the one delivered earlier that day, with **ASC** on the lid. With the butt end of her crutch, she pulled the box out and brought it to her feet. It was much lighter before, and since its top was wide open, she could see why. She knelt down and cautiously began to root through the thousands of white packing peanuts inside. For a few moments, she found nothing, deciding whatever was in there was now with Andrea—but then her hand struck something hard. She gripped its slim handle and pulled it from the box.

She stared at the item, perplexed as to why she held on to a foot long wooden stick with a small American flag at the end. It was much like the one stuck in their front yard, the one Kirk had placed there for Luca.

Upstairs, the front door slammed shut.

Donna yelped and stood up, dropping the flag back into the box.

Slow, steady footsteps shuffled over her head. Heart racing, she swallowed and held her breath, listening to the floor above her creak. The thought of calling out to him terrified her to the core. The feeling was so foreign to her, and she hated thinking the worst of the man she loved for so long. But for whatever reason he had, he wanted her out cold, and whatever it was she had very little desire to find out.

Before she could stop herself, she blurted out, "Andy?"

The footsteps halted. The air around her constricted. The floor right above her groaned…and the achingly slow footsteps turned, heading for the basement door.

Donna crept toward the bottom step, candle held out in front of her.

One by one, he descended, his footfalls heavy and forceful.

Something trickled down the stairwell wall to her right.

She looked up and screamed.

By the time Andrea was halfway down the steps, Donna had backed away until her back hit the couch. She dropped her crutches, and searched for a way out. The door-less laundry room was to her left, and the tiny two-foot-wide window near the bar to her right.

When his shoulders and head appeared, Donna realized it was too late for the both of them.

Blood dripped down the stairwell walls like crimson tears as he ran his fingertips across them. From his legs up, dozens of tiny American flags protruded from his nude body, their wooden sticks pressed deep into his muscles. Dozens more had been jabbed into his shoulders, standing out of his arms like tree limbs. Several dangling between his legs. Two out of his ears. And two more from his eyes.

He grinned at her with blood-stained teeth.

"Andy," she whimpered. "What did you...*do?*"

He sang, "*O say can you see! By the dawn's early light!*"

"*Andrea!* What have you done?"

He hit the bottom step and stumbled onto the basement floor. "*What so proudly we hailed!*" He crept toward her.

Panicked, Donna bundled up her crutches and swung them. Andrea easily wrenched them from her grip and tossed them away. Tears rushed down her cheeks. "Stop it! Leave me alone!"

"*At the twilight's last gleaming!*"

Despite the pain, she stumbled backwards on her boot as he reached out toward her. "Andy, please! Please stop—"

"*Whose broad stripes and bright stars! Through the perilous fight!*"

She turned away to run, but a blood-soaked hand reached out and seized her hair. She screamed and struggled. Andrea shoved her forward. She grunted in surprise as she was driven into the wall, her face smashed against the window. The candle dropped from her grip and rolled across the floor, near the blood pooling at his feet.

Andrea brought himself close. Donna could feel the bell end of the flags pressing against her back. She whimpered as he leaned in.

"Don't you see, *caro*? Don't you see the rockets' red glare? The bombs bursting across the air?"

She shook her head. "Please—"

"*Look!*"

Through her tears, she peeled open her eyes.

Outside, the fireworks from the adjoining neighborhoods exploded in copious brilliant colors. They danced and dived across the sky, illuminating their street with every burst. She screamed.

Several bodies were littered across their front lawn. A few of them she didn't recognize, but the faces of Nathan Horning and Father Kirk brought more tears and screams. Much like Andrea, each body was stuck with dozens upon dozens of small wooden flags. His face down in the grass, Horning's rear end was sticking straight up in the air, with layers of flags sticking out from his back and behind like patriotic corn stalks. Kirk has been rendered nearly unrecognizable, with a handful of wooden sticks jutting out of his stretched open mouth. His throat bulged thick with intrusion. In an instant, they were all gone, then another bright bloom in the sky and they were back.

Donna struggled, but Andrea held her tight.

"Don't you see, *caro*?" he rasped. "Don't you see? This is the land of the free…the home of the brave. Everyone out there? They all got what they wanted. *Whatever* they wanted. It was their birthright, yes? Me?" He gripped her neck tighter. "I dreamed the dream. I wanted it all, just like them. I wanted *my* American Dream."

"Andy—"

"And you took it from me!" he screamed, blood misting on her back. "You all took it from me!"

"Please," she moaned. "Please, Andy… I'm so…so sorry."

"*Sorry?*"

"I'm sorry for never telling you about Luca! I'm sorry for- for never telling you about Kirk and I!" She pressed her head against the cool glass of the window. "I will never forgive myself for what we did."

He leaned closer. The flags jutting from his eyes appeared on both sides of her head. "You lied."

"Yes, I lied, Andy. I lied, and I can never take it back. But you still had a son. You were still his dad—not Kirk. You raised him! He's yours."

"And now he's dead, just like his father."

Donna wept at his words. Whatever happened to her husband, the man she spent so many wonderful decades with, was too far beyond reason—beyond sanity. She couldn't be sure the thing behind her was even human any longer.

"It's so beautiful," he whispered. Outside, the fireworks display continued, illuminating the carnage on the front lawn. "Just a world of possibilities out there. For everyone…including me."

She felt his free arm reach up, and he moaned as he slowly pulled the flag from his right ear. He yanked her head away from the window, and into her vision came the wooden stick. Thick, gelatinous blood caked its end, and what hadn't dried dripped onto the carpet.

"I have found my dream, *caro*, the book showed me. I have found it…and I wish you to be part of it."

The stick descended toward her eye.

"*Per favore, caro.* Be my dream."

She grabbed his wrist, pushing away with everything she had.

"*Molto molto.*"

Despite her struggling, the stick continued to inch closer, and before she knew it, the blunt, bloody end was scraping at her cheek. Andrea's harsh breaths filled her ears, his flags waving at both sides of her face. She screamed and screamed. His breaths grew louder. She closed her eye as the stick rubbed against her lid.

Trembling, she dropped her left hand from his wrist, then reached up, took hold of the flag jutting from his eye and pushed.

Andrea immediately dropped the flag from his hand and screeched. Donna spun around to face him. He had dropped to his knees, pawing at the wooden stick that was now jabbed deeper into his head. She attempted to sidestep, but there was still no way around him. From the shelf of the liquor cabinet she grabbed the neck of a whiskey bottle, and before he could stand, she swung it at his head. The heavy glass shattered, its amber contents splashing across the room. Andrea grunted and fell backwards. The pain in her leg forgotten, she bent down and grabbed the still lit candle.

Andrea slowly sat up. He looked at her and blinked over the wooden sticks. He smiled, blood dripping from his gums. "*O say does that—*"

She pressed the candle to his chest. In an instant, the liquor caught fire, and a moment later, Andrea began to scream. He dropped to the floor and writhed in pain, quickly spreading the fire across the carpet. The malodorous liquid which had splashed across the walls and couch went up in flames. Before it could spread to the staircase, Donna leapt over her husband. She stopped, then pulled a picture of Luca from the wall and crawled up the steps, away from the blaze below.

***

Hours later, while police and firefighters spread across the street, working to contain the blaze, the basement below continued to burn. The fire ate at the furniture, melted the TV screen, and blackened the carpet, reducing everything the Riccis had both held dear to glowing ash.

But high on the bar, as the flames chewed through its aged oak top, the catalog and its glossy black cover and white block letters remained untouched.

Story Notes:

Long before I wrote fiction, I was a musician, and like most musicians, I was subscribed to probably a dozen different guitar and musical equipment magazines. The problem is when you're a subscriber to those publications, they often sell your information to numerous other companies, who in turn send you their catalogs without your prior knowledge. Most of the time, I didn't really care, but there was one catalog in particular I didn't want. It was a from a very small custom guitar company, who shall remain nameless. I thought their instruments were butt-ugly (Hey, I'm a Gibson guy. What can I say?) and I didn't want to keep getting their catalogs in the mail. But no matter what I did and no matter where I moved to, I kept receiving mail from them. They simply wouldn't go away. Years later when I started to write fiction, that little piece of my past kept coming back to me and poking me in the shoulder. I didn't know exactly what to do with it, and like many initial story ideas I get, I placed it on the back burner to simmer. Sometimes they sit there for little while, sometimes for a long while, but eventually, if they're not a completely shit idea, they'll form into something. All it takes is time and inspiration.

That inspiration came in the form of the Fourth of July.

Much like the magazine, nearly everywhere I've lived, someone in that neighborhood has taken it upon themselves to place little American flags at the corner of everyone's yards for American Independence Day. That sauce, combined with the sauce already simmering, with a dash of the loss of the "American Dream" and everything came together like a beautiful Sunday gravy.

CELEBRITY MEAN TWEETS

Gabriel Thomas wanted to get this over with as quickly as possible.

Sure, he'd seen the videos, had seen his friends, co-workers and highly respected professionals degrade and essentially make complete asses out of themselves. All for cheap laughs from the swinish multitude of Middle America. All for the perfect internet clickbait video. Hell, even *Saturday Night Live* (a show he'd hosted twice now, back when it was still funny) didn't give two shits about their ratings anymore. It was all about going viral. Who could top one another with something more outrageous or shocking? It was goddamn pathetic.

But he was nothing if not pathetic himself these days.

Like a lost child, he allowed himself to be strung along through the bowels of the studio. As if *he* needed the assistance. He'd been in this building dozens of times, had starred and even guest-starred on several of this network's dramas and sitcoms, many of which were older than this zit-faced intern who guided him. Normally, despite their strict instructions to not speak to the talent, these kids would neglect their duties and spend their few precious moments with a movie star gushing about how much they adored their work. Lines of dialogue would be quoted poorly, tears occasionally spilled, then Gabe would sign whatever used napkin they had folded in their pocket and off he would go to the lights of the soundstage, away from the fawning, hungry eyes of those he pretended to do this profession for.

But that didn't happen. Whoever this kid was barely looked back at him as he led Gabe through the darkened, musty guts of the Midtown Manhattan high rise. He probably had no idea who Gabe even was. Kids these days. If you weren't YouTube famous, then who gave a shit? Did those internet twits study their craft in Moscow *and* at Juilliard like him? Did they have nearly one hundred and thirty acting credits to their names? How many Oscars and Emmys did they win? How many millions had they earned over the last three decades?

Oh, who the fuck was he kidding? Both schools barely remembered him as an alumnus, most of the shows he starred in were canceled, both of the little gold men on his mantle were now property of his household dust bunnies, and much of that seven-figure bank account now belonged to his ex-wife Madison and his estranged daughter Piper. In Hollywood terms: A Has-Been. Which is exactly why he was going in front of cameras to read mean comments about himself from the online trolls. All in the name of good-natured fun.

He didn't want to do this, had zero intentions on having a 'good time', as his publicist had instructed. Anne, the overpaid cunt, told him it would be good for the rehabilitation of his image. Gabe heartily disagreed. It was humiliating and utterly demoralizing and everything he detested about the entertainment industry. He wasn't some goddamn clown ready to twist a string of rubber into a puppy-shaped balloon. He was an actor—an *artiste*. And despite the fact he knew his career was on the wrong side of fifty, and in maybe ten more years he would be supplementing his income with signing glossy eight by tens at fan conventions, he still took himself very seriously. If he didn't, then where would he be? Hawking dietary yogurt like Jamie Lee? Cheap insurance and pizza like Shaq? Worse yet, doing voiceovers for straight-to-video cartoon features? No, his dignity wasn't ready to decay quite yet. So here he was, ready to put on a happy face and read the awful shit some basement-dwelling nobody vomited out on social media.

"Almost there, Mr. Thomas," Zit-face said, not turning to face him.

Gabe rolled his eyes. "Yeah, I know. Thanks a bundle."

He'd been plenty rude to countless pages and interns in the past, but this one remained stoic. The kid didn't react at all. He kept silent as he pushed on through the vacant, whitewashed hallways toward the stage area. Maybe Gabe was losing his touch? Along with his thinning hair, everything seemed to be falling away around him and washing down the drain. How much time did he realistically have left? A decade? Less? He'd seen what had happened to men his age in this business. Leading men became character actors. Young studs became fathers, then grandfathers. The big screen releases became streaming exclusives on your TV. Even one of his best buddies Kurt Russell was playing Santa Claus these days. Fucking pathetic. Eventually they're all found dead with a needle in their arm or their pants around their ankles and a belt tight around their throats. Thankfully, he wasn't one for mind alteration, and the kinkiest he ever got was a finger or two up the ass by whatever nineteen-year-old was currently blowing him for a walk-on role in his next film.

A few more turns and the stage door at the end of the hallway yawned open like a waiting mouth. Zit-face stopped just before the doorway. Without making eye-contact, he placed one arm behind his back and lifted the other in an *after you* motion. Without so much as a thank you, Gabe stepped inside.

As quiet as the walk in had been, the small studio was bustling with activity and commotion. Beneath the low ceiling, the stage crew was hustling back and forth, moving ladders and snake coils of thick black wiring. Men in expensive suits anxiously paced back and forth with phones pressed to their ears. The gaffers kept busy adjusting the overhead lighting.

The door slammed shut behind him, making Gabe jump.

Though he didn't recognize a single member of the show's staff, he all too well knew the woman who trudged his way from the other side of the room.

"Where the *hell* have you been, damn it?" Anne snipped. The angrier his publicist got, the stronger her Brooklyn accent became. "Christ Almighty, you're twenty minutes late! We don't have all day to wait."

"Nice to see you too, Anne. Lovely as always."

She shifted an iced coffee from one hand to the other. "Don't get smart with me, jackass. I know for a goddamn fact the limo dropped you off out front at six on the dot. It doesn't take but five minutes to hop on the elevator and get up here."

Gabe sighed. "I obviously had to stop and sign a couple of things. You know, give the people what they want and all that." In truth, he barely remembered even leaving the limo and entering the building. He recalled exiting the lobby of the hotel and waiting for the driver to open his door, but the rest was a blur.

Anne barked out a sharp laugh. "My ass. We both know you stopped signing stuff ten years ago. Don't bullshit a bullshitter. You were dragging your Tom Ford's the whole way up here, weren't you?"

"No one drags their Tom Ford's, Anne. Would *you* do that to two-thousand-dollar shoes?"

"Look here, *Gabe*. Whether you appreciate it or not, I bust my ass every day for this godforsaken, thankless empire. I've worked *extremely* hard to maintain this level of respect from my clients all the way up to those cheapskate studio heads and beyond. And I developed that stellar reputation because I keep my promises. All I expect from my clients—aka, *you*—is that same level of professionalism and respect. If you ever want your career to get back on the right track, I expect you to keep your promises and to be where I tell you to be, when I tell you to be. Got that?"

Gabe rolled his eyes so hard it hurt. "Yes, mother."

"I worked my tits off to get you on this show. Even your worthless manager, Robin, couldn't pull this off. So show me a little appreciation, huh?"

"*Those* tits?" He pointed at her blouse. "I'm fairly certain my hard work bought *those* for you."

It was Anne's turn to cast her eyes skyward. "Indeed, and Mark thanks you greatly for them."

"How's your husband doing these days, by the way? Still putting up with your…infidelities? Or does he even know?"

Anne rose a quizzical eyebrow. "You're one to talk."

Leaning in, he whispered loudly, "Stop with the innocent retorts, sweetie. Why do you think I'm getting divorced again?"

"And who do you think is trying to fix this mess, you sociopath? You're *this* goddamn close to getting Me Too'd." Anne squared her shoulders, refusing him any gain over her stature. She was the only person in the business who he allowed to speak to him this way. And to be completely honest, it kind of turned him on.

She took a deep breath, composing herself. "Listen. Gabe. I'm working day and night to help repair this mess you've made. That's literally my whole job: to make you look your best. Now, I can't do said job when you're showing up to work late with the very same attitude that's gotten you where you currently are. The last two years have been an utter shit show. Help me help you out of the grave you've dug."

Sighing, Gabe nodded. "Yeah. Sorry. Won't happen again."

"There. See? Was that so hard?" She gestured behind her toward the small stage. "Look, I get it. This sucks. Nobody wants to do this stupid shit, but it's just about the best thing you can do for your public persona right now, and let's face it, it's currently about as low as it gets. Between the fights on set, your public temper tantrums, and an ugly divorce, you're lucky they're even letting you do this. You hear me? They didn't even want you to be on an internet show to poke fun of yourself. I stuck my neck out for you. Now go stick your neck out for me and take a few well-deserved jabs to that bloated ego of yours. Whatever fans you still have left will love it."

Gabe wanted to puke, but he swallowed the bile down and gave the woman he shilled out a small fortune to his best smile.

"Perfect." She glanced at her phone. "We don't have time to get you to the makeup chair. Did you bring your kit with you?"

"I did, but..." Gabe lifted his hands in confusion. Sure, he always brought his makeup kit with him, but he'd be damned if he could remember what the hell he did with it. He could have sworn it was in the limo with him. Right? He tried hard to remember the ride over, but the entire six block trek was a blank spot in his brain.

"It's fine. You look decent enough." Placing her hand on his back, she gave him a hard shove forward. "Now go give the people what they want."

"Yeah, yeah, yeah..."

"And don't forget to laugh. Nobody likes a stick in the mud."

With a wave of his hand, he strode purposefully toward the other side of the cameras. The one place he controlled in his life. The environment where he could shine brighter than the stage lights. His domain. Painful as it was to admit, Anne was right. If this was the way to get the adoring public back on his side, or at least the start of it, then fuck it. Read a couple of half-ass jokes and he'd be back in his penthouse hotel room in an hour. Hell, maybe Anne would join him. After all, he did pay for those tits...and it had been a bit since they'd been in his hands.

A small, rotund man with thinning, side combed hair waddled Gabe's way. Sweat waterfalled down his face. "Gabe, it's a pleasure—"

"Gabriel, please."

The man stopped, visibly embarrassed.

Gabe paused and shook his head. "Gabe is fine. Sorry. My apologies."

The man's face lit up. "Hey, I'll call ya' whatever you want, Mr. Thomas—Gabe. You're the talent here. I'm just glad you finally showed up."

"Yeah, sorry about that. Traffic and all."

"Hey, it's no problem." He reached out and they quickly shook hands. "Harold Portis. I'm the show's producer and creator. Why don't we make our way over the stage and get started, yeah? We're already running behind schedule."

Gabe fought the urge to tell the little man to go fuck himself.

He once again found himself being escorted forward, this time through a small crowd of camera operators and union staff, all of whom didn't lift an eye as he passed. They stayed busy, making final adjustments to their equipment before they set to record the show. He suddenly felt like a head of cattle being led to slaughter. His annoyance and reluctance quickly shifted to apprehension. He wasn't used to being ignored. It felt awkward. What little good mood and determination he had talked himself into was quickly dissolving.

Portis led him to the small stage near the back wall. In the middle of the small riser was a simple padded armchair. Behind it, the backdrop was painted in a light baby blue, decorated with the black silhouettes of disembodied heads, all mouths open and laughing.

The producer handed him a cell phone. "Everything is already loaded on the screen. Just read them one at a time and swipe for the next one."

Gabe took his seat and eyed the four separate cameras surrounding him in a tight C. "Yeah, sure. By the way, how many of these—"

But the man was already gone, disappeared into the black behind the stage lights.

A moment later he heard someone yell, "Action!"

His call to start was so sudden, he was caught completely off guard. He wasn't sure what to say. Despite being a well-versed performer, improv was not his strong suit. He awkwardly gave the cameras a wave.

"Hey, everyone! Gabriel Thomas here." He lifted the phone. "Going to read some Mean Tweets here today. Hopefully you guys aren't too terrible to me."

Just as the producer said, the first Tweet was waiting for him on the open screen.

"All right. This one appears to be from @HoosierDaddy-1987. It says, 'Someone! Quick! Tell me Gabriel Thomas is a great actor. I need a good laugh today.'"

The unseen crew behind the cameras began to chuckle.

Gabe fought the urge to roll his eyes, using that energy instead to croak out a laugh. "Not bad, not bad. You got me. Thank you, internet rando."

He flicked to the next screen and eyed the small black text. "Okay, then. This next one is from someone named @tickytacksmickysmack. Quite the name there, Ticky Tack. It says, 'Ike Turner has had bigger hits on Tina than Gabriel Thomas has had in his whole career.'"

Chuckles from the black beyond the stage rose to a laughter.

Pursing his lips, Gabe managed an honest to goodness laugh himself. It was wrong as hell, on so many levels, but that didn't make it any less funny. He suddenly found himself relaxing, slouching into his chair. Hell, if this was as bad as it got, then maybe he could handle this after all.

He flicked to the next screen.

"@gayforpizza14 says, 'I've seen Kiwi's with better heads of hair than Gabriel Thomas.'"

Gabe should have been pissed. His hair had been a point of contention for over a decade, trying every remedy he could short of paying for hair plugs or toupees. Yet, something about the brazenness of the statement made him guffaw. Once again, those he could not see laughed loudly, making Gabe laugh harder.

He looked up at the cameras, grinning. "Go fuck yourself, @gayforpizza14."

Off to the side, Anne stepped into view and nodded, shooting him a thumbs up.

"Y'all are going to have to come harder than that to get at me." Feeling loose, Gabe flicked to the next screen.

"What's next? Okay. @slavetotherind says 'Had Gabriel Thomas managed to keep his dick in his pants, his hands to himself, and stayed faithful to Madison Kramer, he'd still be married and not another statistical Hollywood failure.'"

Despite the uproarious laugher that exploded throughout the room, Gabe's joyous mood popped like a swollen balloon. He read the Tweet to himself once again, slower, making sure he read what he read correctly. He did indeed. His grip on the phone tightened. His tongue pressed hard against his teeth. After a few long moments, he took his eyes away from the phone and glanced up.

Those standing in the dark behind the camera set up were now visible, as were their smiling faces. Each one of the twenty or so people were cackling like a pack of wild hyenas. Doubled over in laughter. Holding on to one another for support. Even Anne was leaning forward, hands on her knees, eyes closed as she laughed hysterically. Her iced coffee was now spilled across the floor.

Gabe failed to see what was so goddamn funny.

But…that was the name of the game. The comment hurt, but that was the point, right? To cut him deep. That one hit a nerve.

Forcing himself to not chuck the phone across the room, Gabe gave the cameras an exaggerated grimace. "Ouch, y'all. A little much, but okay."

He sighed and flicked to the next screen.

"This next gem appears to be from a user by the name @YoMammaSuxSocksInHell. Cute name. They say…" He paused, pre-reading the Tweet before speaking it out loud. His mouth went dry. "Nope."

A voice, one who belonged to that producer, yelled, "Read the line!"

The stage lights seemed to glow brighter. Hotter.

Gabe squinted. "No, I don't think I will, guy."

The producer stepped out between the cameras and screamed, "*Read the fucking line!*"

Swallowing hard, Gabe glared at the man before returning his eyes to the eight inch screen in his hands. "Whether on her knees, on her stomach, or on her back, Gabriel Thomas's daughter Piper Anya has seen more pole than a Daytona stripper."

Like a time bomb, the room detonated with uproarious laughter. The camera men fell backwards in their chairs. The lighting crew tugged at their hair. The producer and Anne were both on the floor, rolling around in the spilled coffee like hysterical children. It was the funniest thing that had ever been spoken, and Gabe didn't get the joke. It was one thing to shit on him. He was a big boy; he could take it (mostly). But something he wouldn't tolerate was any bad mouthing of his estranged daughter. They stopped speaking seven years ago, and he hadn't seen her in person in nearly five, but that didn't make a damn bit of difference. That was his flesh and blood.

Seething, he stood and swiftly smashed the phone on the concrete floor before him. "Enough!" he screamed. "If this is the kind of crap you're going to have me read, then I'm fucking done!"

Their laughter continued unabated. If anything it rose in volume, seemingly filling every square inch of air.

"What the hell is wrong with you goddamn idiots?"

Before Gabe could storm away, a hand gripped his shoulder from behind. Off balanced, Gabe yelped as he was pulled back down into his seat. "Motherfucker, let me go!" He tried to turn his head upward, to the dead man who dared lay a hand on him, but the man's other hand smacked down onto the top of his head, holding it firmly in place. Gabe attempted to tear the hands off of his being, but at fifty-three he wasn't at his peak strength, and whatever punches and clawings he lashed out with would have been met with laughs by his younger, more virile self.

The stage lights grew brighter. Hotter.

While his younger self wasn't around, the laughter before him continued on uninterrupted. The producers, the stage crew, the camera operators—all pointed directly at him in merriment. A sideshow freak on display. Then, one by one, they each produced their own cell phones from their pockets and began to read out loud.

"Gabriel Thomas, stop forcing your terrible, non-acting ass on the world, you has-been loser."

"Once named People Magazine's Sexiest Man Alive, Gabriel Thomas's only claim to fame these days is sleeping with underage girls and then getting away with paying them off before heading to court. How many bastard kids does this guy have running around he doesn't know about?"

"The Bush's Baked Beans dog is a better actor than Gabriel Thomas, and that dog is mostly CGI."

"Did anyone ever hear that song Gabriel Thomas had on the radio in the early 1990's? I've heard better noises coming out of two cats fucking than what he thought he was doing behind a microphone."

Anne called out from behind her screen, "Gabriel Thomas's prick is so small he uses a contact lens for a condom." She glanced up at him, grinning. "I wrote that one!"

Laughter erupted like a nuclear bomb throughout the studio.

The overhead lights grew brighter. Blinding. White hot.

"I'll fucking sue you!" Gabe screamed, his neck bulging. "I'll sue you all! You can't do this to me! Let me go this instant!"

Someone continued, "I've said it a thousand times but I think it deserves to be said once more: Gabriel Thomas can eat shit and die. Who does that loser think he is?"

"Hey!" he shouted.

"Has anyone else seen Gabriel Thomas's daughter's leaked nudes online? I've beaten off to those pics probably as many times as her father has."

"You goddamn bastards!"

"Question: who's old as dirt, twice divorced, a terrible father, and is now stuck doing voice-overs on fast food commercials? Gabriel Thomas, that's who!"

Tears streamed down Gabe's cheeks, red hot and angry. Unable to physically stand, he gave up fighting the person holding him down, so he sat there, fuming, embarrassed, belittled. Each insult was like another hand grabbing him and yanking him down from the top of the ladder. No one had ever spoken to him with such irrelevance, such animosity—at least not to his face. And it was utterly devastating. His reputation had been shattered into a million gleaming shards. For the first time in his life, he wanted to die.

"Gabriel Thomas should just kill himself and rid the earth of his narcissism. What a miserable douche."

"Stop," he whined, defeated. "Please..."

From out of the back, two figures strode out into the mounting crowd. Gabe squinted against the intense light. He could barely make them out, but that didn't lessen his shock to see it was his ex-wife and teenaged daughter. Madison, in all her plastic enhanced glory, grinned like the Cheshire cat as she pulled her phone from her purse.

"If anyone ever wondered what it was like to be married to a self-absorbed misogynist like Gabriel Thomas, imagine Donald Trump with less money, less hair, and an even tinier dick. And much like the former game show host, I spent my time married to him fucking everything that moved."

Gabe felt the color drain from his face. Though he had no room to be mad, it was still a massive blow. He could barely breathe.

Behind him, the man holding him down laughed hysterically. His voice was deep and resonant.

Beside her mother, Piper Anya waved sarcastically to her estranged father as she glanced down at the electronic device in her hands. "One cock, two cock, three cock, four; white cock, black cock, yellow cock, more. Big men, skinny men, men who can ball; it doesn't matter, I've had them all!"

Gabe choked back a sob. "Jesus Christ, Piper!"

"Maybe," she carried on, "if Gabriel Thomas was a better father and didn't spend his down time away from movie sets banging his co-stars and traveling the world without his family, his daughter would have grown up normal and not felt the need

111

to act out and show her pussy on the internet for the world to see." She looked up to her father with a shrug. "Seems like more than four hundred and eighty characters, right? *Who* could have written such a terrible thing?" She then lobbed the phone over her shoulder and began to shriek out a long string of forced laughs. The massive crowd around her, which appeared to be growing by the second, joined her. Their guffaws filled the air like a dense smog, filling his lungs and gagging him.

When it seemed like the overhead stage lights couldn't grow any brighter, they exploded. Sparks erupted and rained down over their heads. In a matter of seconds, the room lit up with dozens of small fires. Gabe screamed as the crowd of faceless, cackling onlookers went up like dry tinder. Each one combusted in yellowed flames, the fire eating at the clothes and hair. But you'd never know anything was happening to any of them. They continued to laugh at Gabe, each one taking turns hurling social media witticisms his way.

Gabe howled at the intense heat as it surged around the stage. His tears now forgotten; he went back to fighting against the person who insisted on keeping him immobile. Much like the burning bodies before him, the man behind him laughed on. Gabe wrenched his neck sideways, giving him a quick glance at the backdrop. The joyous painted faces were now alive, animated and hollering, their heads thrown back, open mouths adding to the din. Above him, the flames had now crawled up to the ceiling, and within them, hundreds of tiny mouths snickered.

The man behind him leaned close to his ear. "What's the matter, Gabe? Can't take a joke?"

"Please let me go!" Gabe howled. He beat at the man's hand on his shoulder. "You motherfucker! Let me go! I don't want to die!"

"*Hmmm.* Such a stark difference between *want* and *need*. Nobody wants to die, but some of us need to, am I right?"

Gabe tried to slide down the front of the chair, but the man's fingers dug into his shoulder and broke the skin. Gabe shouted in pain. The grip on his head tightened, those forceful fingers pressing into his scalp. "Let me go! Let me go, goddamn you!"

"And where would you go, Gabe? Where *exactly* would you go? According to the public, nobody wants you around anymore. Is there truth in their words, Gabe? Is there genuineness in their pleas? Is there Accuracy?" He yanked Gabe up hard and sat him back down on the chair. Gripping his crown, he moved Gabe's head slowly side to side. "Just look at them. Look at all of them, Gabriel Thomas."

The heat burned his eyes terribly, but he managed to keep them open. And what he saw was madness.

Gone were the walls and constraints of the room. What he saw was an expansive landscape of jagged rock and sand, of trees and rivers, of skies and sickly ground, all ablaze in a red-tinged inferno. For as far as his eyes could see, smoldering figures stood before him. Thousands. Millions. As their skin flaked off and their blood thickened into a cascading paste, they still held onto their phones. Blackened bone hands gripped tight to the devices as they continued to spew their insults his way.

Gabe gave up struggling. As soon as he did, the man behind him let go. Blood dripped down his forehead and into his eyes.

"Look at them, Gabe," the man said. "That's your adoring public. They love you. They're showing you just how much."

Gabe couldn't take his eyes off of them. "I'm dead...aren't I?"

"A commuter bus hit your limo head-on on the way to the studio. Nearly ripped the whole vehicle in half. A shame, really. Your daughter was actually going to call you today and see about getting dinner. She wanted to get the wheels going on making amends. Oh well, right? You never really liked her anyways."

A shudder rippled through Gabe's heaving chest. "I deserve this, don't I?"

The hand that once held him down now lightly patted him on the shoulder. "Live like a shithead, die like a shithead."

Flames now overtook the stage and slithered up the legs of his chair. The churning sky above darkened. Gabe let his head drop backwards, and he finally got to see his companion.

"Come on, Gabe. Don't take yourself so damn seriously. Learn to take a joke."

As the flames raced up his legs and onto his chest, Gabe finally opened his ears and listened to their words. And what he heard made him laugh. Hard.

Story Notes:

I've always been a big fan of the roasts Comedy Central puts on every year, where comedians stand in front of a large crowd and make fun of each other for two hours. Normally it's a good time. But the times where an actual actor or musician comes on, it seems a bit touchier when the jokes come down on them. While many seem to be able to take a joke, I've seen plenty who can't, and that's always bugged me. Why did you sign up for such an event if you knew ahead of time it's probably not going to be for you? It's why I wish they would just stick with actual comedians as the roasters, but that's a whole other conversation.

That's where the initial idea for this story came from. After watching numerous internet videos of actors reading the mean, hateful messages written about them online, there always seem to be a few who can't just laugh it off. They take themselves far too serious, and that's always bugged me. I wanted Gabriel Thomas to be one of those types. I had only intended for this to be a flash story, somewhere between five hundred to maybe a thousand words long, but the story refused to let me quit early. It came out far darker than I originally planned as well, but I think that adds to the story's dour mood.

ECHO

Patton Bell didn't exactly make a habit out of waking up in strange places. He wasn't much of a traveler, didn't care for sleepovers as a kid, and when it came to those rare times he found a woman who agreed to be intimate with him, it was always at his house. Call it a quirk, call him eccentric, he didn't care. He just preferred familiar surroundings.

Which made waking up on a beach so utterly confounding.

His face planted in bone dry sand, he lifted his head with a gasp. There was no immediate shade, allowing the severe, blistering sunlight a direct path to blind him. Covering his eyes, he groaned and rolled over. Beneath him, the sand warmed his backside through his shirt and shorts. He opened his hand and looked out between his fingers. Beyond his toes, a vast, turquoise ocean artlessly crashed against the beach. Gulls swept through the air, while others hopped delicately across the golden sand, picking at dead fish. Wiping the warm granules from his face, Patton blinked rapidly and let his eyes adjust to the unexpected scenery. His heart immediately kicked into overdrive.

Where…where the hell am I? he thought. *I hate the goddamn beach.*

Confused, Patton stood on uncertain knees and glanced in both directions. The beach wasn't terribly long, both directions stretching until they curled and disappeared beyond sight. That wasn't what bothered him most. Save for the flocks of birds, he appeared to be the only one there. He spun around, expecting to discover a chain of hotels or at the very least a bungalow. Instead, he was unceremoniously greeted by copses of palm trees and the thick, dense jungle beyond.

"Hello!" he yelled, his voice cracking. "Is anyone there?"

Birds squawked. Waves crashed. No one answered.

His heart really began to pound. His breaths came in short gasps.

"Hello! Please, someone help me! I don't know where I am!"

Wind gusted through his short-cropped hair, and despite the harsh heat, he shivered uncontrollably. He turned back to the sea and scanned the waters, hoping to find…something. Maybe a shipwreck or a boat or a plane—anything to make his nausea dissipate. But there was nothing. Only blue. His head spun, vertigo washing over him.

Think, man, think! Did you go anywhere last night? Were you drinking? Did you go anywhere other than work? Did you pick up food? Did you talk to anyone?

The answer for all of these was obviously no. He rarely ever did anything but work and sleep. He didn't travel, didn't have many real friends, rarely dated, and mostly ate by himself. He should have still been back home in Central Pennsylvania. Not…here…wherever here was. Tears streamed down his cheeks.

"*Someone! Anyone! Help!*"

When he finally received an answer, it wasn't human.

Patton quickly turned back to the jungle at the sound of a bark.

A large dog was standing at the tree line. It appeared to be a husky, but mixed with something shorthaired, maybe a pit bull or a lab. He knew nothing about dogs, and that lack of knowledge froze him in place as the animal took a few tentative steps toward him. Its tail wagged vigorously as the dog barked once more. The dog drew a few steps closer, its short brown and white coat shimmering in the sunlight. Patton weighed his options. He could run down the beach, the dog seemed lean enough to catch him quick. He could also make for the water, but there was no telling what bigger creatures lurked beneath the surface, so that was out.

Another step and another bark.

Patton balled his fists and swallowed, readying himself for the attack—

—but the dog turned and bounded toward the jungle. It looked back at him and barked once more before disappearing into the trees.

Several minutes passed before Patton could unclench his hands.

***

Unable to comprehend any of this, he decided to keep himself busy and walk the length of the beach. He had to know how long it was or where it ended. At the very least, he had to know if he was trapped on an island. For all he knew, civilization was a short walk away. But after hiking nearly the entire day, he circled right back to the very same spot he had woken up on. He was indeed on a small island. He kept close to the water, keeping an eye on the jungle beyond. There was no telling who or what hid in that darkness. He wasn't quite ready to find out.

Though he still had an immeasurable amount of questions, his walk offered him a few hard facts. The island appeared on its own, not part of any visible archipelago. There was definitely no shipwreck, as he had yet to discover anything washed up on the shore, nor had he seen any sign of human life outside of his own footprints. He sat back down in the sand and stared at the horizon.

The water beyond the shore was endless.

Maybe he was dead, passed away in his sleep? Maybe this was Hell?

I had always imagined the afterlife would be a lot less blue, he thought, rolling his eyes miserably.

He felt something approaching him from behind.

Patton spun around, only to find the dog again. The beast gingerly crept toward him.

"Go away!" he screamed, thrashing his arms. "Get the hell out of here, you goddamn mutt!"

The dog let out a pitiful whine and loped back into the jungle.

The day dwindled down, and the sky darkened with an orange haze. Unable to cope any longer, Patton Bell whimpered as he lay down on his side. He closed his reddened eyes. It was a long time before sleep took him.

***

The sound of breathing startled Patton wide awake.

He sat up with a gasp. The wind and sun beat on him simultaneously, both confusing him greatly. He blinked away the sleep, and then suddenly remembered where he was. He had hoped he would have awoken to solid ground and concrete and windows and hot take-out food. Instead, there was only this living nightmare of water and heat, both infinite.

Something leaned close to his ear and sniffed.

Patton jerked sideways. The same big dog stood next to him, its dripping wet nose tasting the air between them. The mutt was much larger up close, its light blue eyes trained on him with curiosity. It was lean and strong, and not at all appearing to be starved. Patton imagined others like himself becoming a meal to this feral beast. He sat there nervously as the dog inched closer.

When it got too close for comfort, he screamed, "Get out of here!"

The dog hopped away, scared, and bounded back toward the tree line.

Short of breath, Patton rubbed his temples. The involuntary shaking was back.

Behind him, the dog belted out another bark.

Patton stood with a groan and faced the animal. The dog stood halfway to the jungle, watching to see if Patton would come after it. It turned its head toward the trees, then back to him, its paws excitedly stomping in place. It took him a moment to realize the creature wanted him to follow. In truth, that was the very last thing he wanted to do. There was absolutely no telling what was hiding in the dark of the underbrush, ready to ambush him. He'd only been here for nearly a day, and even though he was fairly certain he was the lone biped, there were most certainly other animals somewhere in there. Hungry ones.

The dog woofed and stamped the ground.

Steeling himself, he eventually mumbled, "Fine, I'm coming," and trudged toward the jungle.

A happy whine and the dog took off into the trees.

By the time he reached the shade, the dog had nearly disappeared, bounding several yards ahead through the brush. The air was significantly cooler inside, which he would have to keep in mind when he no longer wanted to sleep in the open, and it was thick with pungent aroma of moist vegetation. He kept his head on a swivel, painfully aware of every sound around him. Birds disbursed at his presence. Spider monkeys dashed through the branches. Rodents scattered into their earthly holes. For a moment, he imagined having to actually eat any of these poor animals to stay alive. His stomach both growled and churned at the thought.

Eventually he found the dog, as it stopped and waited patiently for him to catch up. It whined and trotted toward a small opening in the trees. Holding his breath, Patton slowed his pace before carefully walking inside.

It appeared to be a small camp, very obviously made by another human. The small area had been cleared away of brush, creating a small, semi-protected living area. Various homemade tools and bowls littered the soft, wet grass, nearly everything carved and shaped from wood or palm leaves. Small piles of animal bones were stacked near the far corner. Near the center of the camp was a fire pit, unused in some time.

Patton froze. *Oh my God...*

On the other side of the ashes was a man.

Patton couldn't see his face, as his head was turned in the opposite direction. Holding his breath, he crept closer, staring at the man's emaciated chest for any breathing. Lying flat on his back, the man's nude body was covered in large, angry red splotches. Long, ratty hair was splayed in a ruddy halo around his head, and his face was nearly swallowed in an unruly, chest-length beard. The dog sat near the fire pit and whined.

A twig snapped under Patton's foot.

The man abruptly coughed.

Without thinking twice, Patton rushed to the prone man and knelt by his side. The welts were much worse up close, as was his odor. The man reeked of old sweat and emptied bowels.

Patton touched the man's ice-cold shoulder. "Hey, man, are you okay?"

The man sucked in deep, painful breaths, his body trembling.

"Holy hell, I can't believe I found someone else here!" he continued, teeming with excitement. "This is so unreal."

Slowly, the man turned his bearded face toward Patton.

Patton responded with a gasp. He collapsed on his ass and scrambled away.

The man stared dead-eyed at Patton—

—and those dead eyes belonged to him.

Despite the uncountable months of wild growth, there was no mistaking that face, nose, lips, or those dark green eyes. It didn't matter if they were aged or caked in sores. He'd seen that face in the mirror the last thirty-three years. It was *him*, staring at *him*. He didn't know how or why...but there he was. Feeling sick, Patton turned and vomited into the ash pit.

The dog trotted over to the dying man and laid next to him on the ground. A pitiful whimper escaped its throat.

The man who looked like Patton lifted a shaking hand and gently scratched the dog behind its ear. The dog leaned into him.

Still staring at Patton, he whispered, "My Echo..."

A moment later, his arm dropped limply.

***

With bated breath, Patton stared at the dead man who held more than a passing resemblance to him. He tried to tell himself it was just the light or maybe a trick of his muddled mind. Whatever the case was, he wanted to get as far away from this place as possible. He stood and stalked back toward the beach.

Hot, wet tears burst from his eyes. He didn't want to do this anymore. As far as he was concerned, whoever was playing this sick joke on him had won. They broke him. Good for them. He was every bit as weak and pathetic as everyone always said he was. Great. Wonderful. Point officially proven.

Now send me back home!

Halfway back to the beach, he realized the dog had not followed him, and for whatever reason, this upset him. He took a deep breath and angrily stomped back to the camp.

By the time he got back, the body was gone.

Only the dog remained, panting and happy to see him.

***

He was never there. He was never there. He was never there.

Patton repeated the mantra as he stared at the empty indentation in the grass. He knew it wasn't true—he had *touched* the guy—but he wasn't quite ready to admit he was losing his mind. Not yet anyway. That would be saved for when all hope was truly gone.

He was never...there...

When he finished pacing, he gathered himself and began to stuff items from the camp into the pockets of his cargo shorts: a long, jagged stone, a couple of sticks which had been carved into eating utensils, and a few small bowls fashioned from large tree leaves. He also took a large branch that had been sharpened into a spear. He had moved past his initial panic. Now hunger was dominating his thoughts. Did he actually think he could spear something and kill it? Absolutely not. But it was that or starve to death, and he wasn't about to go out like...that other guy...who *definitely* wasn't real.

Feeling more confident with a weapon, he walked on through the jungle.

The dog followed his every step.

Patton had never considered himself a dog person, or really even an animal person, at all. His parents never owned any pets while he was growing up, and that trend continued after he moved out for college. The closest he came to having an animal was his ex-girlfriend's cat, Riot. She was a long-haired tabby, covered in various shades of beautiful brown and yellow fur, and though he was reluctant with her at first, she eventually grew on him. Cats were mostly self-sufficient, much like Patton, which was probably why his ex was still his ex. He didn't think about her much, but he often thought of Riot and wondered how she was.

Dogs were a whole other world to him. Unlike cats, they were in constant need of attention, love, and companionship. They depended on humans for everything—the very opposite of himself. But, after nearly two days of isolation, he quickly realized he didn't want to be alone. He hated to admit it, but the company, even if it was a slobbering mutt, was strangely comforting. He glanced down at the dog.

The dog panted happily at his feet.

Patton nodded. "Come on, Echo."

***

He didn't stay famished for long.

Hunger was a strange thing. It could drive someone to do terrible, desperate things. Patton had never gone hungry in his life. He was well fed, eating whatever he wanted whenever he felt. But here—wherever the hell *here* was—there were no fast food restaurants, delivery services, or late night runs to the convenience store for soda and potato chips. It was him and Mother Nature, and he intended to not let her get the best of him.

And there was Echo as well.

As much as it pained him to admit it, the dog had begun to grow on him. His size normally would have intimidated Patton, but Echo turned out to be quite the companion—and quite the hunter himself. While Patton struggled to catch anything the first few days, Echo effortlessly stalked, tracked down, and killed his own food. He had no idea how long the dog had been stuck on the island before he got there—*Maybe he came with that...other guy*—or if someone had taught him how to hunt, but Echo did what he had to do to survive.

What impressed Patton the most was how the dog was happily willing to share his findings. At first, Patton wasn't sure what to do with the small varmints and lizards. After a few days of living on the beach, he had decided to make a home out of the camp. Even if they were *used*, there were too many amenities left around to ignore, including the fire pit. It took him nearly an entire day's worth of cursing and yelling while rubbing sticks together over a bed of twigs and dead grass, but eventually he forced the flames to come. He squealed with delight. Watching *Castaway* had its benefits.

And with those fires, he was able to cook his gifts from Echo. Without the benefit of spices, the food was truly disgusting, but he was so happy to put anything into his stomach, he didn't care. And, of course, Echo got his half.

***

What Echo couldn't bring him was water.

After searching the entire island for any sources of fresh water and coming up empty, he worried constantly about the lack of something safe to drink. Luckily, it was raining on a nearly daily basis. There were the bowls left behind, which he placed along the beach in the open air. He had seventeen altogether, and for the most part, they stayed filled. Much like the wild animals he was now consuming, it was an unfamiliar taste he quickly had to acquire.

Echo happily slurped up his share.

***

A month into his island captivity and Patton didn't need Echo's hunting prowess to provide them food. He used sharpened rocks and sticks and had learned how to properly sneak up on his underbrush prey. Three months in, he was getting pretty damn good at spearing monkeys right out of the trees. He didn't feel great about it, innocent and curious as they seemed, but as far as he was concerned, in the long run, it was kill or be killed, and he had no intention of letting him or his furry friend starve. Their stringy meat typically lasted them several days.

When he tired himself of land meat, he and Echo stalked the beach. In his before life, he didn't care for seafood, but that didn't stop him from catching beach crabs. It was hard to sneak up on the little creatures, but he used a small basket he found at the camp made from a bundle of sticks wrapped in palm leaves. The crabs were stunningly bland without butter, but beggars couldn't be choosers. Unfortunately, there were no homemade fishing poles, so there would be no catch of the day.

Like the water, he worried regularly the food would run out. But that never seemed to be the case.

***

It had been several months—who was counting anymore?—since Patton had even thought about home. It was such a distant memory at that point, a dream, a passing thought as he stared out at the horizon every night before sleep. He found he didn't need the comforts of conventional life. A blink and those thoughts went away with the sun. He found he needed very little now. Even clothes had become optional.

A little food, some water, and his dog.

He grew closer to Echo than he ever thought he would. When they weren't searching for something to eat, they were having fun. They went for nightly walks on the beach. On days when it grew too hot to be in the open, they would explore the jungle, looking for any sort of caves or rock walls to climb. They swam together in the ocean, never venturing too far from the shore. Despite being a husky mix, Echo loved to go for a dip. They would dry off on the beach, baking in the sunlight until late in the day. Neither made much noise, which was fine by Patton. He didn't need to speak much these days. The breeze did the talking for them.

At night, while the fire dwindled down to ashes, Echo would curl up next to him, and they would fall asleep cuddling. When the dog kicked and cried out in sleep, Patton would hold him tight until Echo's dreams subsided.

***

Despite popular opinion, Hell wasn't a blazing, crimson inferno led by a fallen demon with a pitchfork. Nor was it leading a quiet life of solitude, destined to die without someone to love.

It was being surrounded by the clearest, crystalline waters…and not being able to drink a single drop.

It felt like it had not rained in weeks, months, but in reality, it had only been four, maybe five days tops. That was truly enough to scare Patton badly. He and Echo had done a reasonably good job at maintaining their rations for the last several months (when they were done drinking for the day, Patton would have to hide the bowls up high so Echo wouldn't completely drain them), and when they went a day or two without rain, it wasn't a big deal. But when two days became four and four became six, Patton began to panic.

On the day the sky finally broke open, he was conveniently asleep. He didn't often take afternoon naps, but he and Echo had worn each other out playing catch on the beach, and when the sun was at its highest, he figured a quick siesta would make him feel better. By the time he woke up, the rain was already petering off. He sat up with a shout, realizing he had not set out many of the bowls in several days. But it was too late, only two of them had been filled. Somehow it had to last them until the next downpour.

Patton only took a few gulps, then happily gave Echo the rest.

More rain would come. It had to.

***

But the drought continued on. Another week had passed since seeing a drop. They still hunted and cooked, but it was getting harder to eat. Without moisture, the jungle became stifling and difficult to sleep in. When the other bowl was drained, he really started to panic. Never in his life did he think dehydration was a possibility. A first world problem, sure, but a problem nonetheless.

Yet Echo didn't seem to mind. The dog was as faithful as he could have asked for, keeping him happy even when it hurt. He cuddled with Patton when he felt sick and drained. He even brought back food when Patton was too sick to hunt. The dog kept him company through his ups and downs, always there with a smile.

***

After ten days with no water, Patton found it too painful to move. Even at night, when the winds were at their chilliest, he couldn't muster up the strength to start a fire. Whatever little bits of food they had he couldn't cook, instead attempting to eat them raw, which resulted in immediate vomiting. He let Echo have at it. It didn't matter anymore. When he was awake, he was battling delirium, which was why he preferred to stay asleep. His body was covered in welts and sores and patches of rashes of which he had no strength or will to scratch.

His time on the island was coming to an end.

He was dying...and yet all he worried about was Echo.

***

Patton awoke to barking. He wasn't sure how much time had passed since he was last up. He could barely stay awake. The wind stung his dried-out eyes. His skin sang a terrible symphony, a song on a daily repeat. The internal pain was minimal, but as his muscles atrophied, he found he couldn't even move, instead taking up residence beside their long-dead fire pit. His clothes were now gone, as he was unable to stand the feel on his raw body.

He tried to call out to Echo, but could only croak. He desperately wanted his companion, but somewhere beyond the trees Echo did all the talking for them.

Eventually, Echo came bounding back into the camp and laid back down next to him. Patton managed a smile.

***

A sharp noise snapped his eyes wide open. He couldn't turn his head, at least not without jarring pain, so he laid there for several minutes, listening. His hearing was rapidly declining, replaced by a low hum somewhere inside his head, but the sound which had awoken him cut through the fog like a train. He swallowed with a dry click.

The sound repeated, growing closer.

Footsteps.

His heart leapt.

Echo bounded into the camp. A few moments later, he heard a gasp.

Patton wanted to scream, to jump up and hug whoever Echo had brought back to him, but he simply couldn't. Despite his elation, it was too late for pleasantries. All he could offer their visitor was a racking cough.

Behind him, the person rushed to his side and knelt down. A warm hand touched his side, sending shivers down his spine.

"Hey, man, are you okay?"

Even though it hurt, Patton's eyes went wide. He knew that voice. He knew that desperation. He tried to speak once more, but another bout of coughing hit him. He gagged for air and felt himself shriveling into nothing.

"Holy hell," he heard. "I can't believe I found someone else here! This is so unreal."

He laid there for a moment longer, gathering his strength. He knew what lay behind him, and even though he should have been terrified, for death and for reassurance, he strangely found peace. He immediately called a truce with the powers that brought him here.

With his last ounce of strength, he carefully rolled over toward the slightly younger version of himself. When they locked eyes, a clean-shaven Patton Bell fell backwards and shrieked.

The dog approached and sat next to him. He reached up and gave his friend one last scratch behind the ear.

Without words, Patton offered the other him both condolences and goodwill on his upcoming journey.

Learn to live and love...my double...my mirror...

"My Echo," he whispered.

His arm dropped to his side, and he closed his eyes.

He knew his dog would be in good hands.

Story Notes:

I was recently asked by my former Italian language publisher to be a part of a charity anthology which benefited local dog shelters in the Milan area. It was called *Animali Fantastici e Come Salvarli*, or *Fantastic Beasts and How to Save Them*. It had a nice mix of Italian and American authors, a few of which were my peers and good friends Somer Canon and Kristopher Triana. When I was asked to write a new story, the publisher stated in their email that though they knew many of us wrote fiction that tended to lean toward the heavier, darker side of horror, they explicitly did not want that from any of us. I balked at the instructions. Surely I can challenge myself and not write straight-up horror for once! But after multiple failed attempts at coming up with something, I got stuck. Perhaps my balking was not warranted after all. I let the story go for a while, but I kept getting this image of a guy and a dog stranded on a deserted island. I didn't know what it meant, but the image remained strong. Then the ending came to me.

    I'm really happy they asked for the type of story "Echo" turned out to be. I knew as soon as I wrote the first few lines, I wanted to go for a Twilight Zone feel. I'd like to do more of this type of writing in the future.

WE BARE ALL

Morty wept as he stared out the window.

At ninety-three, it was how he spent most of his time, alone and afraid inside his ramshackle cabin. These days, his brain was like a kaleidoscope. A reflective mix of anger and sadness, shame and despair.

The one sentiment he didn't feel was hope.

Through a teary prism, Morty sucked down what was left of his homemade sour mash and continued to examine the desolate road beyond his yard. Outside, the midday sun strained to break through the dense treetops, keeping his small plot of wooded land in relative darkness. There were days Morty never saw the sun at all. The gloom was normal—it matched his woeful outlook. Nowhere to go, and nothing to do. He was so close to the end, and there was only so much time before he was finally gone…before they were all gone.

Who would take care of the town then?

His ears suddenly perked up. Morty quickly wiped the thin layer of grime away from his window. He gasped.

"Sweet Jesus…"

A car! An honest-to-goodness car! Driving toward town!

Heart fluttering with excitement, he shifted his interest to the rough patch of hardened dirt at the corner of his lot.

It was time to start tilling.

***

While Karl, Dana, and Deangelo laughed among themselves inside the car, Aaron studied the gaudy billboard as it raced toward them. It was the same one he'd seen a dozen times since they'd passed through Atlanta, only this one boasted a different girl. Different girl, same three block letter words stretching across its hot-pink background:

WE BARE ALL

They must have been produced sometime in the nineties—possibly the eighties—because Aaron was positive hair that big didn't exist these days. Curls and waves so high, so full of Aqua Net, it had to be a health code violation. On this particular poster, the blonde's pencil-thin eyebrows were curled in a coy, knowing stare. Her frosted, glittery lipstick, now sunbaked, could have once blinded unsuspecting drivers.

He leaned forward as it whipped past and became yet another fast-food advertisement on the back side. Brazen anticipation off Exit 11.

"No fucking way!" Dana yelled.

Kurt retorted, "Yes fucking way!"

Aaron blinked away the sunlight and the world came rushing back.

Dana turned all the way around in the front passenger seat to face Kurt. "There's no way in hell you slept with *four* different women in the same night, you goddamn liar!"

Kurt slapped the open seat between himself and Aaron. "Why would I *lie* about that? Daddy don't lie!"

"Whoa!" Deangelo stopped him. With one hand on the wheel, he pointed with a rigid finger, keeping his eyes on the road. "Damn it, Kurt, how many times are you going to keep doing that?"

"Doing what?"

"I've told you time and again, you nasty bastard. Stop calling yourself *Daddy*. It's fucking gross. Last I checked, that was rule number two for this trip."

Dana nodded. "That's true."

Kurt barked out a laugh. "Man, piss on you both. Daddy does what Daddy wants. Just because it's *your* bachelor party vacation doesn't mean *you* get to make up all the rules. You're not in charge."

"That's where you're wrong," Deangelo declared. "I *am* in charge. And, for your information, this is *not* a bachelor party."

Dana raised an eyebrow. "Well, I mean, you are getting married in two weeks."

"Correct."

Kurt added, "And all of us are your best friends."

"For the most part, yes."

"And we're driving all the way down to Florida because—"

"Because it's summer and it's the perfect time to visit the beach and get sunburned with said friends."

"Do black folks get sunburned?" Dana asked, grinning.

Deangelo smirked. "Nah, we just get better looking."

Eleven hours into a fourteen-hour drive and Aaron was fully ready to toss himself out the window. Witty banter could only get you so far, but when the hours roll into double digits and those stories and jokes had been on repeat since junior high, there was only so much a man could take. He never wanted to come on this trip or party or whatever the hell Deangelo was calling it. He wanted to spend the only week he had off this year drinking himself into a stupor. Ever since Kenzie left, it was all he could do to cope with the loneliness. At least he wouldn't be lonely for the next week, thanks to Deangelo. But by no means did that imply he would stay sober.

Another billboard flew past.

"My dude, face it," Kurt said. "It's a fucking week-long beach bachelor party."

Deangelo growled. "I said it's not a goddamn bachelor party!"

Dana cocked her head. "Chesya wouldn't let you have a bachelor party, would she?"

Deangelo sighed and rubbed his eyes. "No. You have no idea the hell I went through to convince her to let us do this. Months of begging, and even after she agreed, she made damn sure to remind me every single day that this *is not* a bachelor party. No partying, no dance clubs, no strip joints. Those are the rules, and I plan to stick by them."

"No strip clubs?" Kurt whined. "We're driving to Daytona Beach, the strip club capital of the South!"

"And we won't be seeing a single one."

Kurt crossed his arms and muttered, "Maybe not *you*."

Dana said, "Man, you're really pussy-whipped, aren't you?"

Deangelo side-eyed her. "At least I have a pussy to whip me. What's your excuse?"

"Me? I'm perfectly happy being single right now, thank you very much. I don't need another sad, nagging woman to control my every move."

"Yeah? How's Carrie doing these days?"

Dana sighed. "I don't know. Haven't seen her since the split. I see no reason to be friendly after the shit she pulled."

"Uh-huh. Can't say I blame you."

Kurt laughed in the back seat. "Take some advice from the best-looking one in this car: stay single. I've never needed a woman to hold me down."

Eyeing him from the rearview mirror, Deangelo said, "I don't think that's your choice."

"Hardy-fucking-har."

While the other two laughed, Aaron remained silent, inwardly rolling his eyes. Kurt's hand clasped onto his shoulder, making him jump.

"You see, Aaron and I, we don't need that shit holding us back. We're grown-ass men, carving out our own destiny, flying our own ships, piloting our own boats. Ain't that right, A-man?"

Without looking, Aaron nodded.

"Damn straight. Don't worry about Kenzie, man. She was a grade-A bitch."

Pinching his face, Aaron angrily turned to Kurt.

Kurt asked, "What? Everyone knows I'm right."

"He's not wrong." Deangelo nodded.

Dana added, "Hate to admit it, Aaron, but for once, Kurt isn't lying...unlike what he said about four girls in one night."

Kurt yelled, "I wasn't fucking lying! It was sophomore year in college!"

"Bitch, I've been with *far* more women than you, and I can say with the utmost confidence you have never slept with more than four women in your whole life!"

This time Aaron actually rolled his eyes. He turned back to the window, letting the blazing midday sun warm his tired face. Outside, the kudzu-covered oaks and maples zipped by in an emerald blur. At least three to four more hours of this shit. God help him, he needed a drink—and fast.

Another billboard approached, this one in faded neon purple. Same girl, but with a few more words posted beneath her.

COLDEST BEER IN GEORGIA

"Can we stop?" Aaron immediately asked.

Deangelo glanced back in the mirror. "You okay?"

"He speaks!" Dana quipped.

Aaron wiped the sweat from his brow. "I want to stop."

"Why?" Deangelo asked. "Need a piss break? I guess I could use one myself. Anyone else?"

"No, I'm thirsty."

"Thirsty? We've still got plenty of water and soda in the cooler."

Aaron groaned. "I want a beer, D."

"Hell yeah," Kurt agreed. "A cold beer sounds great!"

"Man, my black ass ain't stopping in the middle of Nowhere, Georgia for no beer." Deangelo vehemently shook his head. "I'm liable to get fucking shot down here."

Aaron grabbed the headrest and pulled himself forward. "Look, D, I've kept quiet this whole time. Not a peep. I'm hot, I'm tired, and I'm cranky. All I want is a damn beer. That's it. Just one. Is that too much for your best man to ask for?"

Deangelo drew out a long breath through his teeth, unhappy with being cornered. "Man, the shit you get me in to. If I get lynched by some men in white hooded robes, I'm going to come back and haunt your white ass."

"That's fine. I'll just make you watch Chesya and I when we get frisky."

"You mother—" Deangelo huffed, then whispered, "Are you sure this is a good idea?"

"What do you mean?"

Deangelo rolled his eyes. "You know damn well what I mean. We don't need you getting drunk. Sober trip, remember? Rule number three."

The vein in the corner of Aaron's eye twitched. "It's just one drink, D. One and that's it. I swear."

Deangelo shot him a questionable look. "Just one?"

"Yes. Just one. In fact, everyone gets one. My treat."

"Fuck. Fine. Where am I going?"

Aaron pointed. "Exit eleven. Two miles ahead."

Dana eyed him, a small grin spreading across her lips.

Deangelo shook his head. "Well, wherever we're going, they better have a gas station. You can fill it up. Also your treat."

For the first time in a long while, Aaron grinned. "Works for me."

***

Tooty slid the red checker across the board and exclaimed, "King me, old man!"

Albert didn't answer. Sitting across the small folding table from her, he continued to stare down at his feet. His glazed eyes focused on something Tooty couldn't quite see. Beside his rocking chair, old Phil snored and kicked in his sleep.

Tooty waved her hand. "Albert? Are you okay, dear?" When her husband didn't respond, she snapped her fingers, wincing at the arthritic pain in her knuckles.

As if coming out of a dream, Albert lifted his head and blinked. "Huh?"

"Daydreamin' again? I said king me, old man."

Albert nodded, embarrassed. "Yeah, yeah, sorry." He placed a checker piece on top of hers and proceeded to rub the salt-and-pepper stubble across his chin.

Tooty watched her husband a few moments as his mind roamed elsewhere. "Want to talk about it?"

Frowning, Albert shook his head.

She reached out and took her husband's hand, rubbing his thin, liver-spotted skin with her thumb. "It'll be okay, hon."

Albert finally brought his eyes up to meet hers. He shrugged. "Will it?"

Letting him go, she sighed and carefully sat back in her creaky, wicker chair. "I think so. Just got to keep the faith. Without that, what do we have?" She nodded. "They'll come. They'll come."

Giving her an unsure smile, Albert nodded back.

She pointed at the board. "In the meantime, it's your move. Get to steppin'."

Old Phil abruptly woke and lifted his head. Both Tooty and Albert heard it too. A moment later, a car came driving past their house.

Grinning, Tooty couldn't grab the gardening tools quick enough.

***

WE BARE ALL was a much harder place to find than Aaron thought. There were no signs at the bottom of the exit, so they collectively shrugged and decided to take a left and follow the deserted highway. The sun soon vanished, giving way to shady treetops which leaned over the road, covering the sky above. It wasn't long before the highway rapidly soured into a maze of ancient potholes and haphazard pinecones.

Deangelo grumbled. "This better be the best damn beer of your life, Aaron."

It was another seven miles of bitching and complaining before they saw any signs of life. A small clapboard shack sat a few yards beyond the tree line, blanketed in thick gray shadows. They were undoubtedly lost, but Deangelo refused to slow the car, instead hitting the gas with a little more zest. As they passed by, an old man in overalls and no shirt stumbled out of the house. Obviously drunk, he halted next to a dirt patch on the front lawn and watched them drive by. He lifted an arm and waved.

Kurt whistled. "I'll bet that old coot knows what squirrel tastes like."

Dana watched as they sped on. "Yeah...he's probably been with more women than you, too."

"Oh, piss off. Cousins don't count." He paused. "Right? Like, they don't count, right?"

"You're a sick puppy, Kurt."

Deangelo called out, "Hey, Aaron, does this bar actually exist, or are we heading for someplace where you plan to make us squeal like pigs?"

His patience running thin, Aaron's eyes continued to roam the dense forest, searching for anything that resembled a town. Maybe Deangelo was right. Maybe **WE BARE ALL** didn't exist anymore, bulldozed away or left to rot somewhere after years of begging travelers to come observe God's gift to lonely truckers. Unfortunately, a lukewarm soda would have to tide him over until they passed over into the Sunshine State.

A few minutes later, a small wooden sign appeared on the right side of the road.

"Welcome to Prancer, Georgia," Kurt snickered. "Population forty-six."

Dana rubbed her arms. "Seems like a very specific number."

"Are we really about to drive around this place for a damn beer?" Deangelo moaned.

Aaron squeezed the driver's shoulders. "Shut up and drive."

With an exaggerated sigh, Deangelo turned onto the roughly paved road into town.

A few minutes later, the sky overhead opened up as they exited the forest and entered the small community of Prancer. Brilliant sunlight gleamed across the road, bleeding over the dozens of small homes which lined the street. Much like the shack a few miles back, these residences had suffered similar dilapidation. Dwellings leaned in all directions, windows covered in hazy, ruffled plastic, lawns yellowed and overgrown with dandelions and crabgrass. Their owners, appearing no worse for the wear, relaxed in rocking chairs on their front porches. Smoke drifted from pipes. Frail, delicate hands knitted. Tired dogs kicked in their sleep.

"Salt of the earth," Dana muttered.

"Won't be long before they return to it," muttered Kurt.

"Don't be rude. These people have probably never been outside of this town. This is all they know."

Kurt shook his head. "Man, that's fucking depressing." He rolled down his window and yelled, "Yo! Want to come to the beach with us? Sand and bikinis, baby!"

An old couple playing checkers on a card table turned to watch them go. Their eyes grew wide with surprise.

"Jesus," Dana yelled, rolling his window up with the front controls. "Leave those poor people alone!"

"I'm just having some fun. Hell, that's probably the most excitement they've had in years."

Aaron turned back around as they passed. Their game forgotten, the old couple were now both standing and heading down their front steps. Each one held a gardening tool as they headed for a small dirt patch on the front lawn of their home.

Deangelo grumbled. "We could have already been in Florida by now, getting some fresh squeezed OJ at the Welcome Center."

Aaron punched the back of the driver's seat. "Quit your bitching. Look—there's a gas station right up there."

Deangelo squinted. "Looks like the gas station from that movie…the one with that guy who wears people's faces." He steered into the parking lot and pulled up to the only pump on the lot.

Unbuckling himself, Aaron popped open his door. "Tell you what, if they have any extra faces in there, we'll get you a newer model. How's that sound?"

"I would be highly shocked if they've ever even seen a black man around here, much less carried their detached faces."

The other two got out and began to stretch. Deangelo remained in the car.

"You coming?" Aaron asked.

"Hell no! Just pump the gas and let's get the fuck out of here, please."

"Fine."

Upon realizing the gas pump had no credit card reader, Aaron filled the tank and casually strolled toward the small station house. Dana and Kurt followed.

Inside, the fluorescent bulbs audibly buzzed above the rows of dusty shelves. Unlabeled cans of food and various

Georgia-themed knickknacks lined the homemade display racks. Yellowed soda bottles sat inside ancient refrigerators, long out of date, as were the candy bars displayed by the register. The smell of old fried chicken permeated the air. Dana and Kurt eyeballed the items, giggling as they sauntered through the aisles.

Aaron stepped up to the front counter. "He...hello?"

The dirty white sheet covering the back room fluttered open. A wild frock of white hair poked out, followed a moment later by a confused face. With a tangled gray beard and a wrinkled blue T-shirt which read "Been there, licked that," a sleepy looking old man stepped out toward the counter. His eyes were suddenly full of shock, and his open mouth looked just as surprised. Only a handful of jagged teeth remained inside the man's blackened gums.

"Well I'll be damned..." he croaked.

"Hello, sir," Aaron said. "I'm very sorry to bother you, but my friends and I just filled up our vehicle and need to pay for the gas."

The old man rubbed his eyes. "Wait...you boys...came to visit?"

"Well, yes. Only for a bit. We saw the billboards all the way down I-75."

A wide smile ruptured across his face. "You boys goin' to the titty club?"

Aaron cracked his own smile. "Um...I believe it's a gentleman's club, but yes."

Dana and Kurt walked up behind Aaron.

"What's this about titties?" Kurt asked.

"I knew it," Dana said, beaming. "We're going to that strip club, aren't we? I saw the advertisements too."

Kurt put his palms up. "Wait—the bar we're going to is a *strip club*? A-man, brother, I knew I loved you for a reason!"

The old man giggled with glee. "Ah, shucks, you boys are goin' to love it! Biggest titties in all of Georgia! Girls so pretty it'll make you pop a woody right there through your Bugle Boys!"

Kurt giggled right along with the old man. "Holy shit, I love this guy!"

Dana asked, "What if we're not able to sport wood, sir?"

The old man tossed Dana a sharp, mean glare before turning around toward the back room. "Helga! Helga, woman, get out here! We've got guests!"

"What?" a frail voice answered.

"Woman, we've got some fine young men who've come to see the titties!"

A few moments later, the sheet parted, and a tiny old woman shuffled out. Much like her husband, her face was alight with glee. "Well, I'll be! Look at this! Two strappin' young men came to visit Prancer!"

Dana shifted from foot to foot, visibly uncomfortable.

The old man said, "I was just tellin' them about We Bare All."

"Did you tell them about the titties, Harold?" She turned to Aaron, wagging a gnarled, arthritic finger. "Young man, let me tell you, the girls down the street, they've got the biggest and best titties in the whole state. You won't believe it! Those girls are young and pretty and willing to give ya a darn good time, yes, sir."

"Welp, I'm sold!" Kurt gleefully exclaimed.

Grinning, mostly from disbelief, Aaron let his eyes jump from face to face. Never in his life had he heard the elderly speak with such open crudeness. Part of him wanted to laugh along with Kurt, but the whole exchange made him terribly uneasy. He wondered if it was some sort of prank the locals played on outsiders to entertain themselves on the rare occasions someone younger than sixty-five stumbled into town. But the two before him seemed genuinely thrilled they were there.

Aaron said, "Well, it's not so much the, um, the nudity we're looking for, ma'am. We're mostly just looking for a cold drink. That's all."

"You're in luck then!" the old woman declared. "Coldest beer in the state—cheapest, too!"

The old man craned his neck, looking past them to the car outside. "That colored fella, he with ya?"

Aaron raised an eyebrow, expecting the man's jovial attitude to evaporate. "Uh, yes, that's our friend."

Rubbing his bearded chin, the old man nodded solemnly. "Welp, I imagine they'll be happy to see him too. Helga, does that old colored couple still reside on Turkey Hill Road?"

"The Barrys? Haven't seen them in a spell, but I believe so."

Aaron asked, "Excuse me?"

The old man waved it off. "'Tis nothing. Tell ya what, you boys go to the titty bar and have yourselves a grand ol' time. Tell 'em Harry sent ya." He winked. "That'll get ya the special treatment."

"Okay, sure." Aaron was growing more uncomfortable by the second. "Here's thirty bucks for the gas."

Harold shook his head. "On the house, young fella." Before Aaron could protest, he added, "Seriously, go now."

"Well...okay then. If you insist. By the way, where is this place? We haven't seen a sign since leaving the interstate."

The old man pointed out the window. "Up the street there, about three blocks or so on the left. Ya can't miss it."

"Great. Thanks again. You two have a good day."

The three headed for the front door, back out into the heat.

"Thank *you*!" the old man called. As the front door closed, the couple embraced each other with a big hug.

***

They were coming. She could feel them. Could taste their energy and their youthful vigor. She inhaled, their potency coming at her like waves.

Without turning her head, she slowly moved her eyes until she found the others sitting next to her in the darkness.

Quivering, they, too, could feel it. Eternity was ending.

Not much longer now.

***

"That old guy was such an asshole," Dana sulked.

Watching the rows of ramshackle homes crawl by, Aaron wasn't even listening. He was focused on the road, so absorbed in his own thoughts he could barely hear anything outside of his racing heartbeat. The embrace of alcohol was so close he could practically taste it. One beer was all he wanted...maybe two... maybe more.

Shit, he thought miserably. *You've got a problem, man.*

He was never much of a drinker before Kenzie came along. His ex was quite the partier, a social butterfly, and it took her a long time to convince him to break out of his cocoon. He loved his *own* friends—hers, not so much. It always took a few drinks for him to finally feel comfortable around them at bars and clubs. Soon, a few became several. Then several became a dozen. By the time he realized he had a problem, half of every paycheck was being pissed away at bars. He supposed this vacation was just as much for him as it was for celebrating Deangelo's last two weeks as a free man.

Just one. That's it. In and out. Poof. Ghost.

"What do you mean?" Kurt asked. "I thought he was pretty damn funny."

Dana pinched her face in disgust. "He completely wrote me off and kept giving me the stink eye."

"Well, they probably don't get a lot of women down here looking to go to strip clubs."

"But I like women!" she huffed.

"He doesn't know that!"

Deangelo stomped on the brakes. All four pitched forward in their seats. "The fuck did you say?"

Kurt shrugged. "What?"

"Did you say *strip club*?" he spat. "You motherfuckers are about to get me divorced before I even get married!"

"What's the big deal?" Dana asked.

"How many times do I have to tell you chuckleheads? No strip clubs! My woman made it *very* clear. You know she don't play like that."

Along the street, dozens of old people stepped out of their houses, eyeballing their stalled vehicle. While many watched with gleeful smiles, others hurried around the sides of their homes, garden tools in hand. An old woman in a pink floral nightgown hobbled down the sidewalk in the opposite direction. She waved happily.

Aaron leaned forward. "Look, D, I'm buying the drinks, okay? Nothing will show up on your bank statement. She'll never know."

The driver shook his head, unconvinced. "She's going to know, man."

"No, she won't. I promise."

Deangelo sighed. "Aaron, if I didn't love you so much, I would beat your ass right here on the street and give these people something to watch."

Aaron sat back with a grin. "Shut up and drive."

Another block, another round of happy, elderly faces, and the club finally appeared behind a copse of cypress trees. The building was so much smaller than Aaron had imagined, about the size of a large garage. The outer layer of aluminum siding had been sunbaked into a muddy bourbon brown, peppered with patches of copper-colored rust. Dozens of metal signs advertising beer and liquor were posted across the front, some of which Aaron was quite sure no longer existed. The massive neon sign attached to the roof that bared the club's name was turned off.

Deangelo pulled into the small, empty lot and chose a spot near the front door. He leaned forward and stared at the three giant words hovering above them. "Yeah? If I'm going to destroy my relationship, they better fucking bare it all."

"Hell yeah! Daddy likes!" Kurt excitedly leapt out of the car.

Dana rolled her eyes and followed.

Aaron placed a hand on his best friend's shoulder. "It'll be fine. Calm down. It's just a drink. If you don't want to look at the women, then look at me instead."

Deangelo barked out a dry laugh. "Man, if some girl is going to put her chest in my face, I'm sure as hell not going to stare at your ugly ass."

Aaron laughed. "That's the spirit."

"Hey…just one drink. I mean it, that's it. Seriously, I'm worried about you."

Shaking his head, Aaron stopped himself from snapping. He took a deep breath and closed his eyes. "One drink."

"All right, let's get this over with."

They both stepped out of the car. The sweltering southern heat accosted them, instantly making them sweat. A light breeze ruffled the cypress vines, sending an empty potato chip bag spinning across the lot. Other than their footsteps, the town was eerily quiet.

Dana approached the front door. "Is this place even open?"

Kurt giggled. "We're about to find out!" He pulled open the door, and the other three followed him inside.

Unlike the sunlit parking lot, the building's interior wasn't as easily visible. The overhead bulbs were all turned off, and the only light came from the waxy, frosted windows near the front door. The front waiting area was small and cramped, filled with dirty leather couches and padded lounge seats. Metal chairs were stacked on top of tables. The stench of old sweat and liquor buried itself in Aaron's nose, and something about it made him feel at home. The door slammed shut behind them.

On the other side of the dance stage, three faces all turned toward them at once.

Deangelo yelped, throwing his arms across the others. Aaron's skin prickled with nervous energy. Dana and Kurt stepped back toward the door.

Three women sat silently beside the stage. They stood, revealing their scantily clad bodies, minimally adorned in lacy bras and panties. An old man with a long white ponytail stood up straight behind the bar against the back wall, while another old man peeked out from inside the DJ booth on the far right wall. All five seemed just as shocked to see them.

Aaron called out. "Sorry to intrude, but are you guys… open?"

The woman closest to them pushed her chair back and slowly strolled over. Aaron eyed her curiously. He wasn't generally into strip clubs. He found them gross and uncomfortable and could always feel the eyes of the dancers' boyfriends watching from the back corner. Not to mention the drinks were incredibly overpriced. But something told him this time would be different. Other than the four of them, the club was dead as a doornail. No one to judge his stares—and, boy, was there a lot to look at.

The young woman walking his way could have been a supermodel had she lived anywhere but the backwoods of South Georgia. Her hair was impeccably done, long chestnut waves steadily flowing into loose curls across her pale, freckled shoulders. Much like the billboards miles back, her lipstick was bright and glossy, with light flecks of glitter accenting their plumpness. Aaron did his best not to glance down, but he had to admit, the pervy old couple at the gas station weren't lying. The other two women had sashayed up behind her, a blonde and a redhead, both equally as gorgeous and out of place.

With a grin, the brunette took Aaron's hand in hers. "Sugar, for you…we're always open."

The lights suddenly snapped on above them. Dozens of smaller bulbs exploded across the wooden walls, showering the room with bright, fluorescent neon. A small whine of static came from the speakers, and a moment later, Metallica's cover of "Turn the Page" came echoing out. Spotlights blazed, illuminating the small, glassy stage and the two vertical brass poles attached to it. Above, a disco ball whirled to life, dotting the scene with glittery life. The living wrinkle inside the DJ booth gave them all a hearty thumbs up.

Aaron allowed himself to be led past the dusty couches toward the back bar. A quirky smile on his lips, he caught a whiff of the brunette's perfume. He couldn't quite put his finger on the scent, but it was absolutely intoxicating. He turned back and saw the other two women take Deangelo and Kurt's hands, all of them following him back. Kurt was unable to contain his glee. Deangelo, on the other hand, appeared miserable, his eyes flittering across the walls. Behind them, Dana walked by herself, frowning.

When they reached the back, the ponytailed bartender playfully smacked the polished wooden bar top. "Boys, boys, boys! What'll we be havin' today?"

Kurt leaned in over Aaron's shoulder. "Y'all got Yuengling?"

The old man pointed and winked. "Coldest in Georgia!"

Aaron was impressed. "That sounds fantastic. Four bottles, please."

The barkeep's smile faded when he leaned past and saw Dana. He broke open the cooler behind him and took out their ice-cold bottles, handing them each one but giving Aaron two. Aaron handed Dana hers, along with a shrug.

She rolled her eyes and turned her focus back on the other women.

"How much?" Aaron asked

"Oh...fifty cents apiece sound good?"

Shocked, Aaron said, "Are you serious?"

The old man winked again. "For you boys? It's my treat."

"Holy shit!" Kurt laughed. "Daddy says we hit the jackpot in this town! Dirt cheap beer and gorgeous women? Heaven on earth, baby!"

The women giggled and led them back to the plush chairs surrounding the dance stage.

Deangelo leaned into Aaron's ear. "One beer, man. We're gone in twenty."

The brunette glanced back to him with a wry smile.

Aaron nodded. "One and twenty. Got it."

***

Two hours and roughly ten beers later, the four weary travelers were absolutely trashed. Nobody had spoken in over an hour. Instead, they stared intently at the three women gyrating masterfully on the glittery stage. Dozens of empty bottles were scattered about the floor and circular side tables, their owners slumped in the chairs beside them. Kurt appeared to be having the time of his life, whistling and laughing, tossing bill after bill onto the stage. Deangelo, though quiet, had greatly loosened up, a small grin plastered on his goateed face. Only Dana appeared to be having a bad time. Once she recognized the strippers had zero interest in her, she continued to drink and play on her phone. Aaron would somehow have to make it up to her later, but for now...

The music ebbed and flowed, as did Aaron's vision as he tried to focus on the brunette. Her primal scent invaded his senses, rolling like Atlantic waves, splashing, enveloping his every thought. Their eyes were locked onto one another's, unbroken for some time. Another cold beer was thrust into his fist, and a moment later, it was draining into his mouth. Fuck Kenzie, fuck Florida, fuck the beach, and fuck this stupid "not a bachelor party" vacation. *This* was all that mattered.

Tito & Tarantula's "After Dark" twined seductively through the speakers, forcing the brunette to slow her silky movements. Aaron was enraptured. By the time the guitar solo echoed through the room, his beer was empty and his mind was just as gone. He shifted in his seat, trying his best to hide the erection straining inside his shorts.

Fully nude, the brunette lifted her eyebrows and nodded behind him. His vision blurred, Aaron turned his head and located a small side room by the bar. Lights flickered beyond the curtain door. He turned back and playfully pointed to himself. The brunette giggled and then climbed down from the stage. Aaron drunkenly stood and took her soft hand as she guided him away. Just before he lifted the curtain and stepped inside, he glanced back to his friends.

Kurt was already disappearing into another side room, while Deangelo was helping the remaining dancer down off the stage.

While he was being led away, the old bartender casually stepped around the bar and strolled toward Dana. The wrinkled old DJ followed as the curtain fell in Aaron's eyes.

The private room was tiny and cramped, not much bigger than a walk-in closet, and the only light was a small strobe which rapidly flickered above their heads. Before he could speak, Aaron was shoved down onto a wide, circular couch. The alcohol sloshing around in his stomach nearly expelled the moment his

143

ass hit the cushions. He belched and quickly covered his mouth. The single speaker hanging from the ceiling began to play Twista's "Slow Jamz," and the brunette found the easy beat and swayed, swinging her sizeable hips to and fro, her breasts following. Aaron reached for his wallet, but she gently smacked his hand away. Resigned to the idea that everything in this miserable town was free, he let his head fall into the backrest and allowed the music to take him away...

The brunette straddled him and sat on his legs, pressing her ample chest into his face. Her scent overpowered him, smothering him like a warm, wet blanket. Sweat poured down his face and stung his bloodshot eyes. His arms shook. He was unsure what to do with his hands. Every breath shuddered uncomfortably out of his throat. She flipped around and pressed her ass against his painfully constrained crotch. Aaron nearly lost his mind. She leaned back and tossed her soft locks into his face. Her perfume enveloped him. He inhaled deeply as it sent a rush of adrenaline through his body, flaring every nerve. The strobe blinked faster. Aaron closed his eyes, shaking uncontrollably. It was all too much, yet not enough.

Over the music, she whispered, "Do you want me to—"

"Yes!" he cried.

Without thinking twice, Aaron spun on his side and fell backwards onto the couch. Her back to him, she sat on his beer-bloated stomach and then swiftly extracted his cock through his zipper. Her hand was warm and quick, and though he couldn't see her work, it was obvious this wasn't her first time. That didn't bother him—in fact, it only drove him wilder. His legs shook beneath her.

What would Kenzie think? This...is...fucking...insane!

The pressure grew and grew. As he neared the edge, he sat up on shaking elbows and leaned to look around her.

His eyes went wide.

While his cock was in the blur of her right hand, in her left she held a small clutch of glowing blue eggs.

Before Aaron could question what he was seeing, he came. Thick ropes of ejaculate arced into the air. Acting swiftly, the brunette moved her other hand over to catch them. The fresh sperm dropped across the eggs, making their soft blue lights immediately grow brighter.

Aaron opened his mouth to protest, but he instead collapsed backwards, his brain shutting down like an engine.

As darkness overcame him, he heard the brunette shout, "I've got it!"

Two more voices hollered the same words.

***

Aaron awoke to the sound of banging. The strobe light was off, the room now pitch black. He stood on shaking legs and went to put his cock back into his pants but found it was already stuffed back inside. Dazed, he stumbled out of the room.

The main area of the club was much like they had found originally it. The lights, the sounds, the life—all gone. The only movement was from Deangelo. He stood on the far side of the room, angrily bashing a folded metal chair against a closed closet door.

"D...what's going on? What happened?"

Deangelo spun around and yelled, "*You stupid motherfucker! I could kill you!*"

From inside the closet he heard, "Is that Aaron?"

Aaron stumbled toward him. "What...why is Dana in the closet?"

"I don't know!" Deangelo screamed. Sweat poured down his face and neck. "Just help me get the door open!" He dropped the chair and then wedged his fingers into the small gap he had created in the doorframe.

Aaron joined him, and after a few moments of pulling, the lock snapped and gave away. The door swung open.

Dripping in sweat, Dana staggered out and furiously shoved Deangelo. "Why did you leave me, you pricks? I was in there for fucking hours!"

Aaron rubbed his throbbing temples. "Wait...what? Hours?"

"Yes! When you assholes went off for your private dances, those old fuckers blindsided me and hit me over the head with something. I didn't even get a chance to defend myself. The next thing I know, I'm waking up in this fucking hotbox. What the hell were you guys doing in there for so long?"

Aaron shifted awkwardly where he stood.

Deangelo growled and punched the closet door shut. "Did they...?"

She shook her head. "Thankfully, no."

"Shit," Aaron blurted, tapping his pockets. "Where's my phone?"

Deangelo shook his head. "Fucking gone, same as ours."

"Hello?"

They all three jumped as Kurt drunkenly stumbled out from his private room.

"Where... Fuck, my head. Where is everyone?"

"We are leaving! Now!" Crying, Dana ran to Kurt and grabbed his wrist, then dragged him toward the front door.

Aaron and Deangelo quickly followed.

When they stepped outside, Aaron was surprised to discover it was well past dark. Crickets and cicadas chanted, filling the world with their angry, strident songs. Without hesitating, they all jumped back into the car. Deangelo revved the engine, and a moment later, they were peeling out of the empty lot.

"Goddamn it, Aaron," Deangelo yelled, "you stupid, selfish fuck! What did I say—what did I fucking say? I said one beer and twenty minutes! We were already supposed to be at the condo by now!"

Aaron rubbed his tired eyes. "I'm sorry. Please...stop screaming. My head hurts so bad."

"Absolutely not! Sorry ain't going to cut it this time, asshole!" Deangelo began to cry. "Oh my God...what have I done? What have I done?"

"Just...just let me think." Aaron turned to ask Kurt what he had done, but the man had already passed out in his seat, his head resting against the window, snoring.

"D, please get me out of this fucking hillbilly town," Dana moaned. "Please!"

"I'm working on it."

The main strip of town passed by in a flash, as did its elderly residents. Aaron pressed his head against the window to look.

Bathed only in lantern light, the owners of each home stood on their front lawns, cheerfully waving at their car. Below their ecstatic faces, each local held the hand of a small, nude toddler. Some were boys, others were little girls, but they were all caked head to toe in fresh, wet earth. The children appeared dazed and lethargic, their eyes unseeing, as if they had just woken from a long sleep.

Dana muttered, "What in the fuck..."

A gleeful chorus of 'Thank you' and 'You saved us' called out into the night.

Deangelo immediately floored the gas.

***

His arms buried deep in the cold earth, Morty pulled with every ounce of strength his frail body could muster. When her small head finally ruptured the loose dirt, he let go of her wrists and reached beneath her arms. One final pull and Morty carefully extracted his little girl from the ground. In the hole below, the remains of a large, blue egg sat in pieces.

"Jesus, Mary, and Joseph…you're so beautiful. So precious." Tears spilled down his bearded cheeks as he placed her on her feet. He spat into his handkerchief and gingerly wiped the smudges of soil from her pale, expressionless face. "I've waited so long for you."

Behind him, the car he saw earlier screeched around the corner and raced as fast as it could down the narrow highway, away from Prancer.

Morty waved as they passed. "Thank you so much! God bless you!" He turned back to his little girl and hugged her hard. His chest hitched, this time with sobs of joy. "God bless you all."

***

Somewhere beyond the cabin, three feminine shapes raced through the forest on foot. Their eternity had ended. They were finally free.

Before long, they disappeared into the night.

Story Notes:

From the time I was born to somewhere around the time I graduated high school and left home for college, my parents would load up my sister and I in the car every summer and drive eight hundred and fifty miles south from Indiana to New Smyrna Beach, Florida for our annual vacation. If you've read my novel *Cruel Summer*, you know it's a place I am very fond of and have since visited many other times with my wife. I always looked forward to that trip. It's what got me through my school year. But what I didn't look forward to was the twelve and a half excruciating hours in the car, tired, hot, picking fights with my kid sister just to pass the time. (Side note: I remember one time we were on that trip, and at some point, I was digging in my nose with my finger. We hit a pothole in the road, and the force pushed my arm up, shoving my finger deep into my nostril and caused a nasty bloody nose. Good times.) There's a particularly dull stretch of interstate going all the way through Georgia called I-75, and sprinkled all the way down from just south of Atlanta to nearly Tifton were these billboards, just like the ones I described in the story. **WE BARE ALL**. My dad and I would always joke about how old they looked and how every year the signs would still be there, boasting that same couple of seductively enticing women, begging anyone horny enough to stop off at Exit (Insert Number Here). The billboards were so frequent, we figured it had to be some huge, epic strip club where everyone in South Georgia got their eyes filled with cheap sin. But by the time we passed the actual building off its exit, it appeared to be no more than a ramshackle garage, rotting in the Dixie sun. When I got older and started to write, I knew I had to write about that place.

And who knows, maybe I'll actually visit **WE BARE ALL** someday...

UNDERNEATH

For as long as I can remember, it was always there. Now, I say *it* because, even after thirty-four long, sleepless, miserable years of life on this earth, I still have no clue if *it*'s a male or female—nor do I care to find out. I've never actually seen *it*, at least not with my eyes, and I'm fairly certain it prefers it that way. But I've felt it.

Oh, I've felt it all right.

Most people don't remember much of their lives back when they were still in single digits. Hell, most can't remember what they had for breakfast the day before. I, somehow, unfortunately, remember *all* of it. The way its nails lightly clicked on floorboard underneath my bassinet. The way the soft pink blanket rustled around my tiny, swaddled body. Its cold, earthy breath upon my tender flesh. Nobody should remember shit like this. Pleasant recollections of happy faces, of cuddles and tickles, coos and kisses don't exist for me. No warmth or embrace. Instead, from the moment I took my first postpartum sleep, I knew nothing but abject terror.

I believe that's its plan. Its purpose.

By the time I was old enough to talk, I couldn't force a single soul to believe me. Believe me, I've heard it all. Overactive imagination. Too much TV. Attention seeker. Faker. I must ask you, why would I lie about this? What sort of gain would I get in life by telling everyone there was something—some *thing*—that dwelled beneath my bed, and every goddamn night it crept out and fed on my distress? Why would I make that up? I didn't want that kind of attention. I wanted a normal life—a life free of fear and regret. Do you think I wanted to feel it slink beneath my nursery covers, lingering over my body? That I wanted to feel its lips and tongue hover just above my prickled, teenaged flesh? Or its slender, boney fingers tip-toeing up my arms as my husband slept soundly next to me?

Every single night of my life was an unremitting nightmare. No matter where I lived, no matter what bed I slept in, it was always there. I existed solely as its sustenance. My fear nourished it, and the older I got, the more I couldn't handle being food. This had to end at some point. It was either *it* or me, and I'm not a quitter. I was determined to not let the bastard cow me any longer.

When our favorite website had its annual Memorial Day sale, my husband and I decided to buy a whole new bedroom set. Two days later, a half a dozen large boxes arrived at our house, and together, we went about setting everything up. While the memory foam mattress slowly unraveled in the next room, we took to putting together the new bedframe. The four piece set was solid oak, at least two inches thick, and the long side panels that easily clicked into place left only the smallest of gaps for virtually no access underneath the bed. After we finished drilling the support slats across the inside, we placed the new queen sized mattress on its home and decided to call it a night.

Hours later, in the dead of night, a rustling woke me. Beneath us, I heard something knock against the side panel— once, twice, then another time with force. It snarled angrily and prodded at the underside of the mattress. Curious nails scratched at what little outside floor it could reach. After a while, it stopped moving and went quiet.

I smiled, knowing for the first time in my life, I could finally get some rest.

Story Notes:

The credit for this story goes solely to my wife. Katie approaches me fairly often with story ideas, most of which we both end up picking apart because they either don't work or the idea has been done before. But this one was different. I remember her describing this one, and it gave me chills. It was something genuinely creepy, and though most writers would rather not be gifted someone else's idea, I knew I had to write this one. I kept it short, sweet, and to the point. And as I'm writing this, I realize there isn't a single line of dialogue within it.

THE NEGATIVE ONE

Like every weekday afternoon, Carmen rode the public bus on her way home from work. Her stomach growled audibly.

She was very hungry.

Bored from staring at the built-up gunk on the flooring, Carmen eyed the other two passengers. To her far left, sitting on the opposite side, was a young black man. Hood over his head, his eyes were closed, and his head was bobbing, as she assumed he had in a pair of ear buds. To her immediate right, two feet away, was an old, bearded white man dressed in weathered, moldy rags. His dead, glazed-over eyes gazed out the window as he continuously nursed a can of Yuengling. Two more empty containers rolled on the bench next to her. Neither were paying Carmen any mind.

This would be all too easy.

Taking an empty can, Carmen quickly lobbed it at the young man. The moment it struck him in the head, he sat up straight and pulled out his headphones. "*Yo, what the fuck?*"

Carmen whipped her head back and forth, her mouth wide with shock. "Wow! What a dick, right?"

Growling, the young black kid stomped past her. He kicked the other man hard in the shin. "Yo, motherfucker!"

The old man yelped, snapping out of his stupor. "Huh?"

"Don't play dumb, cracka! Why you throwin' shit? You lookin' for a throwdown?"

"W-what?"

The kid smacked the can from the man's hand. "*Don't play dumb with me, bitch!*"

"Hey!" the bus driver yelled. "Calm down right now!"

Yes, Carmen thought. *Yes...*

The old man crossed his arms and narrowed his bloodshot eyes. "Get the fuck away from me, you little nig—"

Before the man could finish his slur, the kid lashed out like a snake and struck him across the cheek. A loud *ooof* and the old man folded, collapsing to the grime-covered floor. Growling a curse, the kid dropped to one knee and, with both fists, proceeded to flatten the old man's nose and cheeks.

Instead of moving away, Carmen scooted closer to the fight.

Closer to the food.

It only took a few moments, but within the violent scuffle, a small spray of glowing red dust immediately rose into the air and drifted her way. She closed her eyes as they converged with her skin and absorbed into her body, steadily filling her belly. When blood burst from the old man's nostrils, the red dust grew brighter and flew quicker, satiating her hunger.

The bus driver floored the break. *"That's it! Everyone off—now!"*

Carmen gathered her purse and stepped around the brawling couple. The door whisked open, and she hopped down the steps onto the street. Inside, the fight was still raging. That was okay. She'd had enough to eat for today.

***

Carmen had no need to take public transit to and from work. She made more than enough to pay for a cab or ride share. Hell, she could even afford a brand new car, paid full in cash. But that would ultimately defeat the purpose.

How else would she feed?

It was near dusk, and the streets were alive with din—sirens, screams, gunshots. Nearly five hundred people killed yearly. Over two thousand filled with bullets. Anger. Hatred. Pride. Negativity.

Philadelphia: The City of Brotherly Hate. The perfect feeding ground.

It only took a little bit each day. That was all she needed daily to survive.

Carmen had no idea who or what she actually was. She certainly wasn't a vampire, as there was no need to suck blood. In fact, she couldn't actually *hurt* anyone. Sure, she could instigate, but something uncanny prevented her from laying a hand on anyone in order to feed. Most of the time, that worked out fine. A fist fight here, a little screaming or a shoving match there, and that was enough. She was certainly no glutton.

She kept to herself as she walked the last few blocks to her south Philly apartment. She had no memory of how long she'd lived there...or why. In fact, she knew so little about herself in general. What was she? Where did she come from? How did she get there? She supposed at the end of the day, when her head hit the pillow and her hunger was sated, what did it really matter? Work, eat, sleep, repeat.

When she approached the front of her building, she overheard yelling. Curious, she took the side alley between her building and the business next door and strolled toward the commotion. Droplets of red dust immediately hit her.

"*What do you mean you can't pay?*" A massive man held a shotgun at a vagrant, who was cowering against the brick wall behind him. "I told you the last time you couldn't stiff me no more, Rocky!"

The homeless man, Rocky, held his hands up in the air, shaking uncontrollably. "I-I-I don't have anything right now, Buck! Honest!"

Carmen crept closer, absorbing the negativity. She didn't exactly need it, but it wasn't a bad dessert.

"Liar!" Buck growled. "I saw you yesterday paper-sacking a fifth of hooch! How'd you pay for *that*, asshole?"

Rocky sighed. "How do you think? I sucked off Mitchy for it—same as last time!"

His bearded face red with anger, Buck pumped the shotgun and lifted it to Rocky's head. "Suck on this, you worthless bum."

Before Rocky or Carmen could react, the weapon erupted, and a second later so did Rocky's head. The man's cranium exploded in a gout of blood and brains, each splattering the brick wall in a dark red splash. Rocky's shuddering hands felt around the ragged, gushing stump of his neck before his body collapsed and went still.

Carmen, too, dropped to her knees, but for a very different reason. Normally, the negative energy would pepper her like grains of sand. This time, the violence so extreme and sudden, the dust developed into a tidal wave of nourishment. The moment it hit her, she fell to her back and let it wash over her. It was like nothing she'd ever felt before. It bored into her skin, filling her stomach like those Thanksgiving dinners her co-workers raved about. It even woke her sex, which she never had use for. The sensation was indescribable. Remarkable.

Noteworthy.

Buck saw her and approached, his gun pointing down. "You say anything, bitch, and I'll end you too, *capiche*?" When she didn't respond, he spat on her and took off down the alley.

Craving more, Carmen crawled over to Rocky's headless body and the pooling blood beneath him. The red surge was gone, but the immense hunger bloomed anew, ruling her actions like a feening addict. She inhaled his blackened neck stump, marveled at the bits of pinkish brain as they dripped down the wall. The smells...the sights...the emotions... It was almost too much to handle...yet she didn't want to let it go. Her hands covered in warm blood, she vigorously rubbed herself through her jeans, moaning louder than the oncoming sirens.

***

As she lay in bed that night, her mind soared. Nothing had ever felt like that, had ever *completed* her. Now that she'd felt it, Carmen knew she could never let it go. She closed her eyes and smiled. It would be so easy.
    This *was* Philadelphia, after all.

***

Carmen could have easily gotten carried away—go *big* or go home—but she decided to start small. To be smart. Start local. South Philly was not exactly the nicest place to reside, but what the hell did she care? All she had to do was feed, go to work, pay her bills, and keep up some normal appearance to not arouse any suspicion. It provided her with all the negativity she could ever ask for. But what she found was there so much more to be had. Yelling and fist fights were one thing. Blood and viscera—those were the Powerball Jackpot of feasts.
    It took her a lifetime to discover this banquet. Bib around her neck, she intended to never leave the dinner table.
    On weekends, she would visit her local Bed, Bath, and Beyond and purchase nearly every set of kitchen blades they had stocked. She would then place them around her neighborhood and the surrounding blocks, hoping for the best. Some days were better than others. She would stalk the alleys, waiting for something to transpire. Sometimes she got lucky and would spot the occasional stabbing or disemboweling in the act, when the negativity and red was at its paramount, but more often than not, her stainless-steel apple seeds would wind up stolen. As frustrating as it was, she got very little from knife wounds. Sure, that initial wave was blissful, but it never gave her that newfound *umph* she craved.
    She would have to get creative.

***

Since she had a perfectly clean background, Carmen was able to purchase as many firearms as she desired (God bless America!), often in bulk. Week after week, she would take her collection of pistols and walk down to the area of Tioga-Nicetown, where brutal gun violence was a way of life, and drop off full boxes on sidewalks and park benches. It didn't take long before air filled with the stench of cordite. A grin on her lips, she would relish the floods of red.

One young man had taken a bullet to his chin, wiping it completely off his face. After the coast was clear, drunk on indulgence, she laid next to him on the pavement as the life bled from his body. Carmen nuzzled him, rubbing her cheeks against his newly opened mouth, and then used the remains of his tongue to rub against her sex. She kept his severed muscle inside her for nearly a week after.

In another incident, she darted toward multiple gunshots and found a middle-aged woman whose stomach had taken the brunt of several close-range shots. Her midsection had been blown wide open, and the woman wailed as she struggled to keep her raw insides from slipping out. Carmen knelt beside her as the red filled her stomach to a harmonious bloat. When the woman finally died, Carmen dragged her patulous corpse to a dumpster. There, she further opened her stomach and slipped her entire head inside the cavity. Her head resting within the woman's hollowed ribcage, Carmen fisted her own vagina and anus until she passed out from exhaustion.

It was the best sleep she'd ever had.

***

Her senses were devastated, ruined, and so were her inhibitions. As she laid on her couch, rubbing her large, swollen belly, she knew she was losing her grip. She was aiding and abetting murder for selfish indulgence, and on a nearly daily basis. Today may have been the worst yet.

There had been an Eagles football game, and when Carmen saw they were losing to Dallas by a large sum, she hurried down to the stadium and placed guns and knives amongst the parked cars. It wasn't long before fans in green and blue jerseys were screaming their way out of the building. When they discovered their new toys, words furiously turned to actions.

The parking lot converted into an ocean of red, and Carmen was thrilled to be without a boat. She had writhed on the asphalt, howling in ecstasy as her stomach swelled and her sex detonated. But it was short lived. Police were plentiful, and the violence ended all too quickly. Carmen was fortunate to have escaped before being seen. The whole thing, incredible as it was, made her realize it couldn't continue. She would have to quit—to be quenched with minor scraps and nothing more.

Outside her window, two homeless men screamed at one another, and a moment later, a glass bottle smashed.

Carmen grinned.

Maybe she wasn't done quite yet.

**

"W-where are w-we?"

From inside the glass booth, behind a locked door, Carmen observed as a dozen filthy bums awoke from their chloroform naps. They stood on shaking legs, their mouths wide with fright, eyes frantically searching for a way out. Outside her booth, the men and women were confined to a white, windowless room. The only exit was right behind Carmen. The abandoned warehouse was so easy to find, it was laughable.

Her whole body buzzed with anticipation.

"Listen to me very carefully," Carmen called. She had to wait a few moments as they screamed at her before continuing. "I'm not going to repeat myself, so listen up! You've all been chosen to participate in a special tournament. How very lucky of you all!"

"*A tournament?*" a toothless woman cried. "What is this? Let us out!"

The rest echoed her sentiment, screaming and crying to be freed.

Carmen spoke over them. "Yes, a tournament! And there's a prize...one hundred thousand dollars!"

That immediately shut them up.

She lifted an open briefcase and showed them the neat stacks of green bills inside. "But only *one* of you get this. The catch is...it's going to the last one standing."

They glanced at one another, shocked.

Carmen pointed behind them. "Inside that box, you'll find

all manner of instruments to aide you in becoming champion. Last one alive gets the money and the key to leave."

Their immense fear was palpable.

She leaned forward. "*Go!*"

It took several moments of hesitation before an old black man dove for the box and extracted a wooden bat. In a blink, he swung it and struck another man in the face. Blood exploded from his nose and flew across the room.

"Money's mine, assholes!"

The room erupted in chaos. While ducking the man's swinging bat, the remaining vagrants scrambled for the box and found their own means to an end. A small woman dressed in a garbage bag swung a dull butcher's knife and struck a man in the shoulder, exposing the yellow fat and pink, glistening muscle beneath. Bright blood bloomed across the floor. An Asian man drew a golf club and struck another man in the legs, shattering his kneecaps like glass. Two women fought over a long screwdriver. The smaller of the two wrenched it away and repeatedly jabbed the taller one in her breasts. In the far corner, an elderly man used a hard rubber mallet to pulp a younger man's face as he straddled him on the floor. He continued to pound until he hit the floor beneath.

Blood flew. Screams soared. Anger pulsed.

Carmen couldn't handle it.

She bellowed her pleasure as the red stuffed her body. She allowed it to consume and saturate her very soul. A supreme feast, if there ever was one. Opening the door, she stripped bare and collapsed to the blood-soaked floor, enabling the madness to envelop her. The carnage swelled, as did her stomach, as both grew by the second. Above, blunt objects were replaced by sharp edges as the remaining few traded jabs and wounds. Carmen used their severed body parts to stuff into her mouth and sex, wanting every inch of her insides filled. She came hard, harder than she ever before, and nearly passed out. She wept with joy.

Soon the screams died, and the room grew silent. Only the elderly black man was left, gore splattered and panting. "Money...key..."

Her stomach the size a beach ball, Carmen lifted her arm and pointed to the booth.

The man left quickly, leaving her beaming, blood-soaked form behind.

***

Miserable, Carmen stumbled home, nearly dragging her feet along the sidewalk. She held her stomach as it bounced with her steps. It was after midnight, and no one would see her blood-covered form as she made her way home.

It was everything she'd ever hoped for and so much more. She didn't think she could hold much more, and that was fine. This was *absolutely* the last time. She couldn't go on like this, so having such an epic conclusion to her gorging saga was something she would not soon forget. Maybe one day, in another city, she could try again. Maybe...

She turned down the alley and shuffled toward the front door. A massive shape stepped out from the dark and shoved her to the ground. The barrel of a shotgun was thrusted into her face.

"Where are they, bitch?"

She immediately recognized Buck, the drug dealer who had blown off Rocky's head. "Who? What are you talking about?"

"Manny, Constance, Jupiter, Granny B! *Who do you think?*"

"The bums?" she asked, grinning.

"Yeah, bitch! My goddamn clients!"

Red dusted off him and hit her stomach. Carmen shuddered painfully. She pointed to the blood on her face and shirt. "Say hello. They're all here."

His neck bulged with fury. "*You goddamn psycho! You killed them? All of them? Do you know how much money you just stole from me? What the fuck is wrong with you?*"

Carmen couldn't stop him. As he raged and struck her with his gun, her belly reacted, bulging bigger and bigger. Her shirt stretched and ripped as it ballooned and grew twice its size. The red blinded her, and soon it would be her undoing.

Buck pumped the gun and aimed, but he wasn't quick enough.

Before she could stop him, Carmen's stomach exploded on its own. A massive wave of red dust exited. Like a swarm of bees, it buzzed and whirled around his body, overtaking him. Inside the crimson tornado, Buck spun and screamed. A few blinks passed and all that was left was a quivering mass of loose innards as they dropped and *splat* on the asphalt.

Fading quick, Carmen watched as the swirling red slowed and began to form the framework of a body. Arms and legs, a head and breasts. When the red dissipated completely, the silhouette of a woman stood silently in the dark.

A woman who looked just like Carmen.

Her carbon copy stared at her blankly for several long minutes before sauntering away without a word.

Carmen closed her eyes, content. She hoped her copy was hungry.

There was plenty of negativity out there for everyone.

Story Notes:

Yeah, I know. That was...wrong. But what do you expect from a story written for an anthology called *Gorefest*? When K. Trap Jones put out an open call for stories for this book, I knew I wanted to write something for it. I didn't have an immediate idea for it, so I went to my notes.

Ideas for stories hit me all the time, but they're almost never fully formed. Typically, they're just snippets of an idea, fragments of a scene, a line of dialogue, or maybe just a title. If I don't have my notebook and pen with me, I'll jot it down in my notes app on my phone. The biggest problem is that I'll type out that line or two and then completely forget about it, sometimes for months at a time. So when I went perusing through my phone, I came across a note that said: Someone who feeds on negativity. I honestly don't remember when I wrote that or what it even meant. I'm sure I was watching a movie and something sparked in my brain. Who knows? But those five words were the catalyst for what you just read. I wanted this story to be unflinching and uncomfortable. I wanted the reader to grimace as they read certain passages.

And yes, the title came from a Slipknot song.

ACKNOWLEDGEMENTS

A major thank you to the following editors for believing in my work enough to publish it (or at least allowed me to strong-arm them into the deed): Ken McKinley, Mircalla Karnstein, Brian Keene, Jarod Barbee and Patrick C. Harrison III, Mauro Saracino, Kenneth Cain, and K. Trap Jones.

Big props to John Brhel and Joe Sullivan for being awesome and giving this project life.

To Trevor Henderson for the incredible artwork.

Thank you once again to Lisa Lee Tone, Tod Clark, and Kyle Lybeck for their eyes and their second opinions.

And much love to my wife and son, Mom, Dad, Sis, Joseph Hunt and family, Mary SanGiovanni, Mike Lombardo and Lex Quinn, Somer and Jessie Canon, Wile E. Young and Emily Rice, Chris Enterline, Kristopher Triana and Bear, Stephen Kozeniewski, Kenzie Jennings, John Wayne Comunale, Lucas Mangum, Bob Ford, and John Boden.

Author Bio

Wesley Southard is the two-time Splatterpunk Award and Imadjinn Award-Winning author of *The Betrayed*, *Closing Costs*, *One For The Road*, *Resisting Madness*, *Slaves to Gravity* (with Somer Canon), *Cruel Summer*, *Where The Devil Waits* (with Mark Steensland), *The Final Gate* (with Lucas Mangum), and *Try Again*, some of which has been translated into Italian and Spanish, and has had short stories appear in outlets such as *Dig Two Graves vol. II*, *Midnight in the Pentagram*, and *Clickers Forever: A Tribute to J.F. Gonzalez*. He is a graduate of the Atlanta Institute of Music, and he currently lives in South Central Pennsylvania with his wife and their son. Visit him online at www.wesleysouthardhorror.com.

Made in the USA
Columbia, SC
24 March 2025